CHASING HELICITY

FORCE of NATURE

ALSO BY GINGER ZEE

Into the Wind

Natural Disaster

CHASING HELICITY

FORCE of NATURE

GINGER ZEE

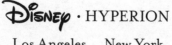

DISNEY · HYPERION

Los Angeles   New York

Copyright © 2018 by Ginger Zee

All rights reserved. Published by Disney • Hyperion, an imprint of Disney Book Group. No part of this book may be reproduced or transmitted in any form or by any means, electronic or mechanical, including photocopying, recording, or by any information storage and retrieval system, without written permission from the publisher. For information address Disney • Hyperion, 125 West End Avenue, New York, New York 10023.

First Hardcover Edition, April 2018
First Paperback Edition, March 2019
1 3 5 7 9 10 8 6 4 2
FAC-025438-19039

Printed in the United States of America

Library of Congress Cataloging-in-Publication Control Number for Hardcover Edition:
2017003037
ISBN 978-1-368-04964-1
Visit www.DisneyBooks.com

This book is dedicated
to my little tornado, Adrian

S he had to escape. The loud music. The louder neighbors. The grilled burgers that were harder than hockey pucks and about as flavorful. The red, white, and blue paper goods the late-afternoon wind kept tossing to the ground. She couldn't take it any longer. Memorial Day in West Michigan was more all-American and annoying the older and more cynical she got.

Helicity caught her mother's eye and gave her a pleading look. Her mother's lips twitched in either a smile or a grimace, but she nodded her permission for Helicity to leave.

Helicity snaked her way across the backyard toward the kitchen. Snatches of conversation reached her ears.

"Got to have been a proud day for you when the Michigan State offer came," she heard Mr. Robison say to her father. "A football scholarship is nothing to sneeze at." His congratulations were edged with envy.

Her father, a large, muscular man with sandy hair turning to gray, gave a slow grin. "It does make paying for college a little easier to manage," he acknowledged.

Helicity paused by the kitchen door and glanced over at her brother. At six foot four, Andy was easy to spot despite the admirers surrounding him. He was a good-looking guy—thick, wavy brown hair, green eyes, and high cheekbones, features similar to her own—but it was his ability to thread a football between defenders and into the hands of a receiver that made him so popular. Thanks to his throwing arm, their high school football team had posted back-to-back undefeated seasons and finished with a top ranking in the state. In their small town, that made him a hero.

Andy saw Helicity looking. He flashed her his crooked smile and raised his can of pop.

Two girls turned to see who'd captured his attention. "It's just his little sister, Felicity," one said. They turned back, dismissing her without another thought.

"Helicity," Andy corrected.

"What?" the girl asked, looking confused.

"My sister's name. It's Helicity."

"Helicity?" The girl gave her friend a look. "What kind of name is that?" Her friend giggled.

It was a fair question. The answer was sweet and a little nerdy. Just like Helicity. Helicity's grandmother had liked the sound and meaning of it. A brilliant woman, Grandma Picossi had studied physics before marrying. *Helicity* was her favorite physics term—it basically means *to spin* in a helical or corkscrew motion. *Helicity*, the word, was an integral part of her thesis and doctoral work. A decorated physicist, she died just before Helicity was born. Helicity's mother insisted on choosing a name that honored her memory. While it was a little strange, Helicity considered herself lucky. The alternative was Doris.

Leaving Andy to his posse, Helicity pulled open the kitchen door and almost ran into Mrs. Van Houten, who was coming out with a platter of watermelon slices. "Sorry!" She ducked in and let her neighbor pass. As she did, her elbow hit a stack of mail on the counter and knocked it to the floor.

"Careful, dear!" Mrs. Van Houten sang.

Helicity apologized again, but Mrs. Van Houten was already closing the door behind her. With a sigh, Helicity picked up the mail. Amid the flyers, catalogs, and bills was a letter from her middle school. It was addressed to her parents, but since it was open, she decided it was fair game. She slid the letter out and scanned the contents.

Dear Mr. and Mrs. Dunlap:

Congratulations! Your daughter will be starting high school next fall. Our guidance office is pleased to inform you of their recommendations for her placement in the science and math classes. College prep, or CP, classes offer instruction at a moderated pace while the more challenging honors, or H, classes move more briskly through the curriculum. The recommendations below are based on careful evaluation of your student's middle school performance in both subjects.

Helicity had been waiting all week to learn if she'd placed in the higher-level honors classes. Like her grandmother, she was drawn to science and math. Unfortunately, those subjects were not always easy for her. She was pretty sure which level she'd be recommended for. Still, her heart fell when she saw the CP boxes checked for both categories.

A thud on the door startled her. Mrs. Van Houten was there, sagging under the weight of a whole watermelon. Helicity let her in.

"Thank you, sweetie." Mrs. Van Houten deposited the melon on the counter with a sigh of relief. "Want to help me cut this up?"

Helicity murmured an excuse and hurried from the kitchen. She had to get away, go to the one place where she could be alone and think.

In her bedroom, she changed out of her shorts and T-shirt into her riding clothes—boots, jeans, and lightweight long-sleeved shirt. She jammed the letter in one pocket and her smartphone in another, quickly weaved her long brown hair into a thick braid down her back, and then sneaked downstairs and out the side door. She ran to the barn in the far corner of the field behind her house. Her horse, a blue-black gelding named Raven, nickered a welcome. Twenty minutes later, Helicity and Raven were galloping toward a distant hill.

Western Michigan is relatively flat, so the hill provided a good view of the area. A well-worn path wound up the side. Raven didn't need direction; he'd covered the ground many times before. When they reached a rocky overlook at the top, they stopped. Helicity dismounted and let Raven wander to a nearby patch of grass while she took a seat on a boulder.

She could see a full 360 degrees because there were so few trees on the hilltop. Her town and others nearby spread around her in all directions—a cross-hatching of dirt and paved roads dotted with a golf course, schools, a sprawling mall, churches, and farms. Subdivisions radiated out from her town's center in ever-widening circles, like ripples in a pond, slowly encroaching on the outlying farmland. On the western horizon, the lowering sun lit up a billowing cloud bank with shades of red and orange.

Helicity picked out the hospital where she and her brother had been born. Other than summer trips to Lake Michigan and a fall weekend here and there in

East Lansing to see a Michigan State football game, they'd rarely left their town since.

Andy is getting out soon, though, Helicity thought. In a month, he'll start training with the university football team. Traveling to games all over the country. *I'll be home alone with Mom and Dad.*

She wasn't sure that was going to go well.

She pulled the school's letter out of her pocket. *Mom hasn't shown this to Dad yet,* she realized. She knew if he'd seen it, he would have made some disappointed comment about her "not reaching her full potential"— among other remarks. She smoothed out the creases on the paper. As she did, a paragraph she'd missed in the first reading jumped out at her.

You can opt to overrule these recommendations and place your child in a higher level. But please be advised that doing so may result in lower academic achievement.

She hadn't realized she and her parents had a say in the matter. Toying with the end of her braid, she played out different scenarios in her head.

If I bump up to honors, I might not be in class with my friends. Worse, I might crash and burn. Dad would have plenty to say about that. Maybe it would be better to just stay in CP. But CP level classes might not get me on track for—

A flash of lightning jolted her from her thoughts. Thunder rumbled seconds later. A sudden wind bent the branches of a nearby tree and teased loose strands of her hair. Raven tossed his head, jangling his bridle.

Helicity moved to soothe him. "It's okay, boy," she murmured. "It's just a little rain, a little thunder." She stroked Raven's glossy neck, glancing back at the storm as she did. What she saw made her pause.

For as long as she could remember, Helicity had been fascinated by the weather. Her favorite television program was whatever was on the Weather Channel. Her heroes were meteorologists and storm chasers. She couldn't tell you much about the conflicts in the Middle East or the starlet on the cover of *People* magazine. But if you needed a detailed five-day forecast, you asked Helicity.

Western Michigan got its fair share of wild weather—lake-effect snow from Lake Michigan, drenching rain, ice storms, heat waves, even the occasional twister. So she'd had plenty of opportunities to observe storms up close and personal.

But what she saw on the horizon was unlike anything she'd ever witnessed.

She took out her phone, tapped to Video, and zoomed in on the gathering storm. "I tell you what, Raven, I'm glad we're seeing this from up here. Because I think anyone near that"—she hit Record—"is about to get walloped."

CHAPTER TWO

The humidity, heavy during her ride up the hill, was only a little better at the higher elevation with the strong breeze. That breeze started feeling more like a jet engine screaming at her back and heading straight into that thunderstorm. She realized she was now feeling strong "inflow"—something she had only read about. Holding her phone with one hand, Helicity plucked at her sweat-soaked shirt with the other. A zigzag of lightning lit up the towering cumulonimbus. It was a split second of incredible natural beauty. She almost crowed with delight, knowing she'd caught the moment on her phone.

A gust of wind freed more hair from her braid. She brushed it off her face with an impatient sweep, but the wind just blew it right back. She ignored it, switched her camera from Video to Photo, and snapped some stills.

Several clicks later, Helicity glanced at the corner of the screen and groaned. Her battery life bar was in the red, meaning it was at less than ten percent. The last thing she needed was for it to die completely. If her dad tried to call and couldn't get through, she'd never hear the end of it.

"Why am I spending my money on that thing," he'd reprimanded her the last time her battery ran out, "if you don't bother to keep it up and running?"

"I just forgot to charge it, that's all," she'd mumbled. "It won't happen again."

He'd snorted. "That's what you said the last time. Maybe if you spent less time with your head in the clouds . . ." He'd thrown his hands up in disgust and walked away, leaving Helicity with her head bowed and her face burning.

I don't know why I'm worried about him calling me, she thought now as she took a few more pictures of the changing clouds. He probably doesn't even have his phone on him.

Unlike most people nowadays, her father detached from his phone the minute he walked through the front door. A general contractor, he built new houses and renovated older ones. He was charming and agreeable with his clients during work hours, but when he was at home and off the clock, he refused to receive or return their calls. "I only have the damn thing because of work," he told Helicity's mother when she questioned that practice. "When I'm here, I'm not working, am I?"

Yeah, no hypocrisy there, Helicity thought sardonically. I'm supposed to be available all the time, but him? Only when he chooses to be.

She sat on the boulder and drew her knees up to her chest. Ignoring the increasingly low battery, she thumbed through the photos she'd just taken. Even on the tiny screen, the images of the clouds and gathering storm made her heart beat a little faster. She'd given up trying to understand why she reacted that way. Fascination with the weather was a part of her. Couldn't change it. Didn't want to.

But she'd learned not to bring up her interest at home. Her father had made it perfectly clear that the topic bored him. "For Christ's sake, the *weather*? That's all she can think to talk about at dinner?" she'd heard him scoff to her mother recently.

Thunder boomed again, closer this time, and louder. Raven gave a snort of alarm. Helicity slid off the rock and moved to the horse's side. "Okay, boy, I hear you. We'll get going in just a few . . ."

Her voice trailed off as she glanced down at the land below. She blinked rapidly, trying to process what she was seeing.

Moments ago, the storm had looked threatening. Now it looked . . . wrong.

The clouds, once a billowing tower of white and gray puffs, had morphed into an overwhelming structure, the dark base of the storm sagging nearer to the ground by the minute. Out of that base, a disk-like wall bulged even closer to the ground. It almost looked like an alien invasion from one of those Independence Day movies. That disk started spinning. The brilliant oranges and sunset reds slowly darkened to pitch-black.

No, not all black, Helicity amended uneasily. She took out her phone and began videoing. *There's green there, too. And it's not just raining. It's pouring behind that storm.*

Suddenly, something clicked in her mind. The wall cloud, the rain, the wind, the greenish color—they all added up to one very frightening possibility.

"Raven, I think we'd better—"

Waaaa! Waaaa! Waaaa!

Her phone suddenly blared. Startled, she dropped it. It landed faceup, showing the message that had popped onto the screen.

> Emergency Alert!

And below it appeared two words that confirmed her fears.

> Tornado Warning.

She snatched up the phone and scanned the rest of the message. Her mouth turned dry when she saw her town listed in the heart of the danger zone.

Her phone buzzed. A text from Andy appeared.

W R U???

She quickly typed:

With Raven! I'm

She was just about to type *safe* when the screen went black.

"What? No! No, no, no!" Helicity clicked the side power button frantically. Nothing. She stabbed and swept the screen with her finger. But it was no use. The battery was dead, the text unsent.

She swore and shoved the useless device into her back pocket. "Come on, Raven, we're out of here." She swung herself up into the saddle and looked at the storm.

The ground below the spinning disk of a cloud was now whirling, too. Slow at first, the spin gained momentum. "Helicity," she whispered. "That's what helicity looks like."

The whirling motion in the cloud and on the

ground magically came together, and suddenly it was as clear as any book, movie, or YouTube video—that was a tornado. Thin at first, the tornado quickly grew in width. Helicity didn't wait to see more. She wheeled Raven about, and they set off down the path.

A foreboding darkness gathered around them. The wind blasted them as they descended, swirling up dusty, leaf-riddled debris from the ground and throwing it in their faces. Helicity squeezed her eyes to slits and ducked just in time to avoid a low-hanging branch.

But she couldn't avoid the hail that suddenly battered them as they rounded the first corner of the twisted switchback trail. The hail started small, about the size of a pea, and stuck in her hair and on her clothes. As they rode, the hail grew exponentially— now falling as golf ball size and then as big as a baseball. One smacked her in the arm, and it stung. "Oww!" she shrieked. She pulled back on the reins, forcing Raven to slow his pace. As surefooted as her horse was, she couldn't risk him stumbling.

"You can do it, boy," she murmured desperately— more for her own benefit than his, for there was no way the horse could hear her over the wind and hail.

She reached forward with one hand to pat his neck.

At that moment, there was a loud crack. A violent gust had snapped a nearby tree in half. The top crashed to the ground directly in Raven's path. With a sharp whinny, the horse reared. Helicity lost her one-handed grip on the reins and flew backward out of the saddle. She landed hard. Pain shot up her spine, making her gasp. Raven took off at a panicked gallop.

"No! Stop!" The wind snatched her weak cry from her lips. Grimacing, she got to her knees and then to her feet. Every movement brought stabs of pain, but she knew she couldn't stay where she was. Too late, she'd realized it had been a grave mistake to try to outrace the storm.

If I'm caught here and the tornado hits . . .

Unbidden and unwelcome, terrifying images of flying branches and uprooted trees assaulted her mind. Her body would be pummeled. She choked back a sob and started running.

She didn't head down the path. She knew tornadoes could strike hillsides as well as level ground, but right now, the nearby open space on the hilltop was infinitely safer than the heavily forested trail hemming her in.

And if I can't make it home, then I want to be there.

Arms protecting her face, she struggled up the trail. She rounded a bend at the edge of the hill and stopped short with a gasp.

Below, the tornado had grown even bigger and stronger, and much more ferocious. It tore through an isolated grove of trees, ripping them up at the roots and hurling them skyward in pieces. A nearby outbuilding blew apart like a house of cards. The debris floated, almost magically, as it swirled with the motion of the storm.

Staying as far away from the few trees as she could, she ran to the boulder and threw herself facedown on the ground next to it, hoping it would offer some protection. She drew in her knees, covered her head with her hands, and squeezed her eyes shut. Hail pelted her back. The roaring wind whipped at her clothes and howled in her ears.

"Please," she whispered into the dirt. "Let me be all right. Let everyone be all right. Please, please, please."

Time seemed to halt as she repeated her mantra over and over. "Let me be all right. Let everyone be all right. Let me be all right. Let everyone be all right."

Suddenly, something changed. The hail turned to heavy rain, and then, as if someone had switched off a faucet, the rain lessened to a drizzle before abruptly stopping altogether. The wind quieted and the air stilled. She opened her eyes. The light brightened marginally. After a moment, she turned onto her back and stared at the sky. Gray clouds gave way to wisps of white and then pale blue.

It's . . . it's over.

Wincing, she sat up. Her tailbone and back felt bruised, her shoulders tight and knotted with tension. She rolled them a few times, testing them for pain, but they were fine. Grit coated her skin, clothes, and hair and filled her nostrils. She was drenched, but as she licked her lips she could still taste dust.

"But I'm okay." Her voice cracked. She cleared her throat and swallowed hard. "I'm okay," she repeated, stronger this time. She stood on wobbly legs, staggered to her boulder, and climbed up. Then she flung her arms wide and, because she could and because it was true, she yelled at the top of her lungs, "I'm okay!"

Only then did she see what had happened to the towns down below.

CHAPTER THREE

When Helicity was little, she'd happened upon the carcass of a dead rabbit. It had been ripped open from throat to crotch by some wild animal, its blood-soaked guts surrounded by soft white fur. That's what her town looked like now—as if the claw of some gigantic creature had torn through it, leaving a horror show of mutilation framed by pristine countryside and farmland.

Mom. Andy. Dad.

Helicity slid off the boulder. Ignoring the lingering pain in her tailbone and bruises from the hail, she ran for the trailhead and continued down the hillside. Her wet clothes clung to her and made her limbs heavy and difficult to move, but she didn't stop. Adrenaline was driving her. When she reached the fallen tree, she scrambled over, shoving aside the branches that grabbed at her arms and scratched her sides and face. She slipped on a patch of rocky soil and nearly fell. But she didn't slow her pace.

Mom. Andy. Dad.

The names rolled through her mind, repeated in sync with her footfalls. The hill trail ended in a small dirt parking lot. It was empty of cars. She swore under her breath, her wild hope that someone would be there who could drive her home dashed.

Mom. Andy. Dad.

Somewhere in the distance, sirens wailed. She ran on, aiming for an overgrown field. Crossing it instead of going to the road would cut the distance home in half. Her boots, so perfect for riding, now made her feet and calves ache. She could feel blisters, hot and painful, forming on her heels, but she didn't stop. She pushed through prickers and scrub and emerged next to the dirt road she and Raven had taken to the hill earlier. She threaded through a rusty barbed wire fence and picked up her speed.

Mom. Andy. Dad.

A few miles outside of town, a police car roared up next to her, its blue lights flashing. "You live in town?" the officer yelled from the open window. Too winded to answer, she nodded. He stopped the car and pushed open the passenger door. "Get in!"

She slid onto the seat and slammed the door behind her. "Mom. Andy. Dad," she gasped as she fastened her seat belt. "I have to find my family!"

He thrust a bottle of water into her hand. "Drink," he instructed her as he hit the accelerator.

She took a sip, coughing as the liquid hit her parched throat.

"Take deep breaths," the officer advised. Sandy-haired, blue-eyed, and muscular, he looked to be only a few years older than Andy. His voice was calm and soothing. "Good. Now, who are you?"

"Helicity. Helicity Dunlap. Please, my family—"

"Okay, Helicity. I'm Officer Pete. I'm taking you

to the high school. The tornado didn't hit it, so that's where everybody has been told to go. It's where your family will be if . . ."

He didn't finish his sentence, but Helicity knew what he'd been about to say. *If they could get there. If they survived. If. If. If.*

They rode in silence after that. Dirt gave way to pavement, and then Pete turned onto the town's main road.

"Oh my God." Helicity sucked in her breath as she tried to process the wreckage before her.

A two-story brick building that had stood for more than a century had been obliterated but for the remains of one wall. Farther on, a row of stately older wooden homes had been reduced to kindling, the contents—furniture, appliances, clothing, photographs—flung everywhere. Uprooted trees had smashed through rooftops and, in one case, landed on a car flipped on its side. Patio furniture, swing sets, bicycles lay wherever the twister had hurled them. Helicity tried to make sense out of what she was seeing.

"Please just get me to my family!"

They rode in silence the rest of the way. Pete parked in the high school's side lot, next to the football field. She leaped out before he even cut the engine. "Helicity, wait!"

She ignored him and ran to the front entrance. Throngs of people, all wearing the same dazed and terrified expressions, pushed in around her. She ducked through them and squeezed into the school lobby.

"Last names *I* through *P*, gymnasium! *Q* through *Z*, auditorium!" a voice said over the loudspeaker. "*A* through *H*, cafeteria! *I* through *P*, gymnasium . . ."

Helicity wove her way through the crowd to the cafeteria. Inside was more chaos. Children cried and whined, ignoring their parents' half-hearted attempts to hush or comfort them. Adults paced back and forth, yelling into their phones, fingers jammed in their free ear to block out the surrounding noise. Many looked frustrated, and Helicity guessed that most of the calls were not getting through because the nearest cell tower had been taken out in the storm. Men, women, and children slumped at the tables, leaned against the walls, and sat on the floor. Some were wrapped in blankets; others held dripping ice packs, bloodstained paper towels, or cups of coffee.

Helicity's eyes darted around, searching faces, praying to see her parents and Andy. She heard her mother's voice and whirled toward the sound, hope surging within her. But it was another woman, calling for a different girl, a girl named Felicity.

Panic replaced hope. She pushed her way deeper into the cafeteria, still searching.

The smell hit her the moment she waded into the sea of people. Industrial cleaner that did nothing to mask the stink of sour body odor, soiled diapers, fresh vomit . . . and fear. She breathed through her mouth, but bile rose in her throat all the same. Her mouth filled with saliva, and she broke out in a cold sweat. Swallowing hard, she fought her body's urge to throw up.

The loudspeaker crackled, making her jump. She couldn't make out the announcement, but suddenly, people surged toward one side of the cafeteria.

Someone jostled her, and she stumbled sideways into a table. Her knee slammed against a hard plastic seat. She saw stars, and then the room started spinning. The smell, the noise, the pain, the humid heat from the crush of bodies around her . . . it was all too much. Her vision narrowed to a tunnel, and she pitched forward.

"Helicity!" Someone grabbed her from behind, spun her around, and wrapped her in a crushing embrace.

The tunnel receded. Helicity choked on a sob. "Mom!" She clung to her mother, breathed in her familiar scent, and let the warm comfort wash over her. "Mom."

"You're safe," Mrs. Dunlap murmured over and over. "Oh, my darling girl. You're safe."

Mr. Dunlap appeared. "Thank God," he said, relief flooding his face when he saw his daughter. He kissed the top of her head and smoothed her hair, then looked around the area. "Wait, where's Andy?"

Helicity stiffened. "Isn't he here with you?"

Mrs. Dunlap pulled back and stared down at her,

frowning. "No. When he realized you weren't in your room, he went looking for you."

Helicity's blood froze in her veins. "What? Wh-when?"

"Right after the emergency alert came over his phone. He grabbed the car keys, said he knew where you were, and took off to get you. I tried to stop him, but . . ." Her mother waved her hands helplessly.

"You're telling me he didn't bring you here?" her father said.

Eyes wide, Helicity shook her head.

Mr. Dunlap's voice took on a hard edge. "He said he texted you. You texted him back, told him where you were, didn't you? *Didn't you?*"

W R U??? An image of Andy's message flashed through her mind. So did one of her phone's screen going black.

"I—I tried. My battery . . ." Helicity couldn't finish the sentence because she was on the verge of tears.

"My God." Frustration and fury warred with concern on her father's face. He turned on his heel and shoved through a group of people to a table with a hastily written sign. *Missing Persons*, the sign said. Mrs. Dunlap grabbed Helicity's hand, and they hurried after him.

"I'm looking for my son, Andy—Andrew—Dunlap," her father told the woman behind the table. "He was out looking for my daughter when the tornado hit."

"And your daughter—"

"She's fine," he said curtly. "My son is the one who's missing."

Now Helicity let the tears come. "Mom, Dad, I'm sorry!"

Her mother folded her back into her arms, but this time the embrace was tight with tension.

The woman's fingers flew over the keyboard of her laptop. Mr. Dunlap came around to her side and leaned forward, his eyes reflecting the screen's glow. All at once, his face contorted as if he was being tortured.

"Oh, God. What is it? What does it say?" Helicity's mother cried.

"Come on." Mr. Dunlap rounded the table. "We have to get to the hospital."

Mrs. Dunlap clutched his hand. *"What does it say?"*

"They found him inside his car." He shot Helicity a look. "What's left of it."

Helicity's mother gasped and pressed her fist to her mouth. "Is he . . . oh, God, tell me he's all right!"

"He's at the hospital. In surgery. Now let's go. Move!"

CHAPTER FOUR

The police didn't want them to leave the school. "It's dangerous out there," Pete informed them grimly. "Downed power lines, potential gas leaks, unstable—"

"My son is in surgery at the hospital." Mrs. Dunlap thrust out her chin. "We're going. You have a car. Take us there. Now."

Helicity had rarely seen her mother so forceful. Pete stared at her for a long moment. Unflinching, she returned the look until he relented. "Hang on." He conferred with another officer and then tossed Helicity a blanket and pulled out his keys. "Okay. Let's go."

They were at the door before he finished speaking. Helicity caught Pete's eye and mouthed, *Thank you*. He nodded and gave her a quick smile.

Helicity and her mother got in the backseat, where Helicity wrapped herself in the blanket. Her father rode up front with Pete. As they drove out of town, they passed pockets of unbelievable devastation. "It's exactly like they always say on the news," her mother murmured. "It looks like a war zone."

Mr. Dunlap didn't speak. He just sat, ramrod straight, and stared out the windshield, unblinking.

Helicity noticed more this time on the slow drive through town. Every vehicle looked as if it had been taken to the junkyard and placed in the compactor, then perfectly placed back on the roads and in the town as if it was on a movie set. Andy had been in one of those vehicles.

A trip that normally took twenty minutes took almost an hour, but they finally reached the hospital. Pete dropped them at the entrance and left to park. They hurried inside.

The scene in the emergency room was as chaotic as the high school cafeteria. Helicity's father bulled his way to the admitting station, with Helicity and her mother close behind. "Andrew Dunlap," he barked at the man sitting at the desk. "Where is he?"

"Are you the family?" the man replied. "You need to fill out these forms." He tried to hand Mr. Dunlap a clipboard with papers.

Helicity's father batted it to one side, lunged forward, and grabbed the man by his shirt. His face was a mask of fury. "I was told my son is in surgery. Either you tell me what's happening right now, or I'm coming around this counter. You understand me?"

"I've got this, Dougie." A woman with dark hair and light brown skin wearing blue scrubs strode over. "Mr. and Mrs. Dunlap? I'm Dr. Suarez, the chief of surgery here. I saw Andy when he first came in. Please come with me."

Helicity's father let go of the man, who shot him a dirty look. Dr. Suarez took the clipboard and led them to an alcove with chairs and a table. "Andy is not in any danger," she reassured them as they sat. Mrs. Dunlap sagged in her chair. "However," the doctor added, "he did sustain broken bones in the accident."

Helicity's mother looked up. "Broken bones?"

The doctor pursed her lips. "Near as the first responders can tell, flying debris shattered the windshield. His injuries suggest he saw the debris coming, flung up his right arm, and twisted away to protect himself." She demonstrated, angling her right arm in front of her forehead and turning aside to her left. "They assume his left hand was still on the wheel, and that the twist caused the car to veer violently. Andy lost control, and the car ran off the road and overturned."

Helicity's father sat forward, tense. "You said he had broken bones. What bones, exactly?"

"The right humerus, here"—the doctor touched an area between her right shoulder and elbow—"and both the ulna and radius, here." She indicated a spot midway between her right elbow and wrist. She cleared her throat and glanced at Helicity. "Forgive me, but I must be graphic. One end of the ulna—that's the outside bone that runs toward the pinkie—was protruding through the skin."

Mrs. Dunlap sucked in a sharp breath and fumbled

for Helicity's hand. Her grip was crushingly painful, but Helicity didn't flinch.

"In such cases," the doctor continued, "immediate surgery to repair the damage to muscle, skin, and nerves as well as bone is necessary. The bones are aligned and then fixated in place so they heal properly."

"Fixated in place? How?" Mrs. Dunlap's voice was a faint whisper.

"With metal plates and screws. Application of the devices is external, if at all possible. Internal if not—which is likely the case with Andy's injuries."

"Internal," Mr. Dunlap echoed. "And then another surgery to take them out?"

"Removal is not always the best option," the doctor said cautiously. "Sometimes it's preferable, even necessary, for them to remain in place. Each case is unique. We'll evaluate Andy's situation as the healing progresses."

"I see," Helicity's father said tightly.

An orderly approached them and handed Dr. Suarez a chart. She glanced at it and then stood. "Andy's out of surgery. He's still sedated, but you can see him."

* * *

It's my fault.

Helicity stared at her brother through the glass. If she hadn't known it was him, she never would have recognized the figure lying in the bed. Cuts and bruises marred his handsome face. His hair was matted and his mouth hung slack. His right arm was encased in a cast from palm to shoulder, the elbow bent and his fingers and thumb free. A tube ran from an IV bag to his arm and another from a small tank to a pair of tubes in his nostrils. Wires connected him to machines that monitored his vital signs.

Mr. Dunlap stared at Andy, too. Then he pounded once on the window with his fist, making Helicity jump. He looked at her. "I'm going to get some coffee. I'd say text me if Andy wakes up before I'm back, but what would be the point? Your phone is dead." He shook his head. "The one time your weather obsession would have actually been useful, and you're off somewhere doing God knows what." He walked away down the corridor without another word.

Helicity's mother rested her forehead on the glass, eyes closed. For a long time, she didn't say anything, though her fingernails dug into the window edging. "Where were you?" she finally murmured. She sounded exhausted. "Why did you leave?"

Helicity had forgotten all about the school letter. Now she dragged the crumpled mess out of her pocket. "I rode Raven up the hill. I needed to go somewhere quiet so I could think about this." She held out the paper.

Her mother glanced at it, then shut her eyes again. "What's to think about? Your teachers have evaluated your abilities and put you in CP. End of story."

Helicity slowly wadded the paper up and shoved it back into her pocket.

"Where's Raven?"

Her mother's query took Helicity by surprise. "What?"

"Raven." Her mother opened her eyes and stared in at Andy. "You said you rode him up the hill. Where is he now?"

Helicity's stomach dropped into her shoes. "I—I don't know. He spooked, threw me, and—"

"He threw you?" Mrs. Dunlap straightened and

looked at her fully for the first time in several minutes. "Are you hurt?"

Helicity reassured her she was fine, just a little bruised. She didn't mention the pounding the hail had given her, though she could feel where the stones had hit. "But I haven't seen Raven since."

Her mother reached out and touched her arm before returning her gaze to Andy. "He'll find his way home." A nurse had entered Andy's room. They watched her fussing over him. "He's young and strong. He'll be fine."

Helicity wasn't sure if she was referring to Raven or Andy.

Mr. Dunlap returned a few minutes later. He fished his wallet out of his pocket and gave his wife some money. "I booked us a room at the Lakeside," he said, referring to a nearby hotel. "It's under your name."

"The Lakeside?" Helicity frowned. "Why do we need to go there? Can't we go home?"

Her parents stared at her. "It was destroyed, Helicity," her mother said at last. "The house, it's . . . gone."

And just like that, another part of Helicity's world

crumbled. She stood rooted to the floor like a statue, unable to breathe, while her parents discussed their immediate plans.

"There's enough cash there for a taxi and some food and necessities, if you need anything tonight. Use the credit card, too, if you have to," her father said. "Keep the receipts."

"What about you?" her mother asked.

"I'm staying here with Andy for now."

"But—"

He cut her off. "Listen, I need some time alone to think. This is going to impact our future. Don't you get that? I need to figure out what we're going to do now." His tone let them know there'd be no argument. He went into Andy's room, closing the door with a firm click behind him.

Downstairs in the hospital lobby, Helicity saw Pete by the front desk. Pete waved her over. "I didn't realize your brother was Andy Dunlap, the football star." He lowered his voice. "How is he?"

Helicity filled him in on Andy's condition. Pete gave a whistle. "Sounds grim. Do they know where he was headed when he was hurt?"

"No." The lie slipped out before Helicity could stop herself. "I mean, they're not sure because he's still asleep after the surgery."

Pete nodded. "Of course. Well, no doubt he'll make a speedy recovery, seeing how he's in such good shape. Still, it's a darned shame. I was looking forward to seeing him play for State." He shook his head.

"Hang on," Helicity said, her brow creased with confusion. "What do you mean, you *were* looking forward to seeing him play? You're not going to write him off just because he's injured, are you?"

Pete looked surprised. Then his expression changed to one of understanding. He laid a hand on her shoulder. "Helicity, you should know that Michigan State might have to rethink their offer to him. They can't afford to waste a scholarship on a player who . . . well, who might not be able to play as well as they had anticipated. If his injuries to his throwing arm are as bad as you describe . . ." He spread his hands wide. "I'm not saying he won't get his chance. But it's possible this accident could affect that chance significantly."

This is going to impact our future, her father had said. *Don't you get that?*

Until that moment, Helicity hadn't gotten it. But now, it was glaringly obvious.

Andy's injuries could end his football career. *He was coming to find me when he got hurt. That means*—she took a shaky breath—*I'm responsible for the end of his career.*

CHAPTER FIVE

Lost in her thoughts, Helicity was quiet on the taxi ride to the Lakeside Hotel. Her mother, too, was silent, the glow of the streetlights casting shadows on her face and making her look older than she was. They pulled into the hotel lot, paid the cabdriver, and got out. Helicity started to walk to the doors, but her mother sank down onto a nearby bench.

"Mom?" Helicity sat next to her and touched her mother's arm. "Are you okay?"

Mrs. Dunlap stared at the ground between her feet for a long moment before finally answering. "I keep replaying what happened back at the house, before the tornado hit. Wondering if there was something I should have done differently."

She shook her head. "We were all having such a great time. Then the town's siren went off and phones started blaring emergency alerts. At first, I thought it was part of a Memorial Day celebration. When people realized what was happening, they panicked. Everyone was shouting, scrambling to find family members, shoving one another aside. Mrs. Van Houten, Mr. Robison, other neighbors, they ran back to their houses. Some people crowded into our basement to wait it out. A handful got in their cars and took off. Andy was one of them. I should have tried to stop him. Them."

Her face sagged and she took a ragged breath. "But I didn't."

Helicity knew she was thinking about what had happened to Andy while he was on the road. She wanted to reassure her, to tell her that nothing she said or did would likely have kept those people, or Andy, from leaving. But the story was coming out of her mother in a rush now, and she didn't dare interrupt.

"I figured the alarms were just a precaution. I

mean, the wind picked up, and we heard thunder and saw lightning through the basement window. Rain, too. Very heavy rain, and then hail. But we've seen that kind of storm before. I never imagined it would actually be a tornado. Then—"

Her mother's voice caught. She cleared her throat and continued. "People say a tornado sounds like a freight train. They're right, it does. But they don't tell you what it sounds like when that train smashes through your house. When the windows burst and the furniture slams into walls and the roof is ripped apart, and you're cowering one floor below."

She raked her fingers through her hair, her eyes darting back and forth as if watching the scene replay in the grass. "They don't tell you that you'll scream until your throat is raw or that you'll smell the stink of urine when the person next to you wets himself with fear. They don't tell you that someone who never goes to church will pray for salvation at the top of her lungs."

Tears leaked from the corners of her eyes and streamed down her cheeks. She turned her head and stared at Helicity with a haunted look. "And they don't tell you how your soul will seize up with all-consuming terror because you have no idea where your children are."

Helicity stared back, frozen in her seat.

After an endless moment, her mother blinked as if mentally shaking herself back to the present. She folded Helicity in her arms and gently rocked her. "Oh, God, I shouldn't have said that."

"No, Mom, it's okay. I— You were all I could think about, too. You and Andy and Dad." She pulled back. "I started to text Andy that I was safe. If my stupid battery hadn't died, he wouldn't have come after me."

Mrs. Dunlap nodded slowly. She wiped away her tears and sat up straight. "What's done is done. We can't change it. We can just help him heal. And to do that, we have to take care of ourselves, too. So come on. Let's get inside."

As they stood, a car drove up and parked a few spots away from them. A group of people emerged and started making their way to the hotel entrance. With their shuffling gaits, disheveled clothing, and blank stares, they looked like a pack of zombies. She didn't recognize them, but she knew at a glance that they, too, were homeless because of the tornado's fury.

Her and her mother's appearances must have conveyed the same thing, for inside, the man behind the front desk greeted them with sympathy. "Welcome," he said. "I'm Ted. I'm so sorry for what you've been through. We'll do our best to take good care of you here." He indicated a computer printout on the countertop. "I just need your last name, then we'll get you right up to a room."

"Dunlap," Helicity's mother said. "The last name is Dunlap."

Ted checked them off his list and handed them an envelope with the room number scrawled on the outside and two key cards inside. "There's a complimentary care package in your room. Snacks and water and other items. You need anything else, please, just call the front desk. I can't guarantee we'll be able to get it tonight, but we'll try. There will be breakfast and coffee served here in the lobby tomorrow morning. And I'm told relief services are on their way."

Helicity and her mother murmured their appreciation before heading to the elevator to find their room. As Helicity got on, she saw a dark-haired girl she knew from school walk into the hotel lobby with her parents. They all looked shell-shocked—expressions Helicity knew she and her mother wore as well.

She was glad the girl and her parents were safe. But she didn't wave or call out. She was suddenly too tired to do more than lean against the wall until the elevator delivered them to their floor.

Their room was a spacious suite with an L-shaped kitchenette with full refrigerator, sink, stove, and dishwasher. The care package the hotel manager had mentioned was on the counter. The kitchen opened into a sitting room with two nondescript armchairs, a flat-screen television, and a pullout sofa bed that someone—the hotel staff, Helicity assumed—had made up for them. A separate bedroom had a king-size bed, a large bureau, and another television. The bathroom was off the bedroom.

Helicity hadn't been to many hotels in her life. Under other circumstances, she would have been excited to be there. She would have scouted out the pool and gone swimming, explored the other floors, and secretly enjoyed the novelty of filling the ice bucket from the machine in the hall. Tonight, though, all she wanted to do was shower and sleep.

"You go on and use the bathroom first." Her mother sat down heavily in an armchair and dug the heels of her hands into her eyes.

Helicity took two bottles of water and two sleeves of chocolate chip cookies from the care package. She put one of each on the table next to her mother and started toward the bedroom with the others. Her mother stopped her with an outstretched hand. Helicity took it and gave it a squeeze. Her mother squeezed back.

In the bedroom, Helicity found packages containing several extra-large white T-shirts and pairs of men's cotton boxers. *In case you need something to sleep in*, a handwritten note on top read. Puzzled at first, it suddenly dawned on her that her only clothes were the ones she was wearing. The anonymous person's thoughtfulness brought a sudden burning lump to her throat.

She took a tee and a pair of boxers with her into the bathroom and flicked on the overhead light. She flinched when she saw her reflection in the mirror. Her hair was a storm-tossed tangle. Her clothes and exposed skin were filthy. Her face and arms bore scratches from her struggle over the fallen tree on the hillside trail. She touched her tailbone gingerly and felt the bruise blooming there. She removed her shirt and turned. Red marks from the hail were already turning blue; they covered her back.

Raven.

An image of her beautiful horse, alone, injured, dying, or dead, crashed into her mind. Other mental pictures, some real, some imagined, followed rapid-fire. Her brother lying in the hospital room. A neighbor praying in her basement. Her father's furious expression. Her mother's haunted face in shadows, her eyes despairing. Andy's car flipped on its side, Andy trapped beneath the steering wheel, Andy covered in glass and blood, screaming in agony, jagged-edged bones protruding from his shattered arm.

Suddenly, the full force of what had happened—and what might have happened—struck Helicity like a punch in the gut. Her breath caught. Her heartbeat pounded in her ears. A choking sob escaped her lips. Then, as it had in the cafeteria, her vision narrowed to a dark tunnel and she thought, I'm going to pass out.

CHAPTER SIX

No. *Don't.*

Helicity doubled over, grabbed the counter for support, and sucked in huge gulps of air. *You're okay. They're okay. You're okay. They're okay.*

She latched on to the words and repeated them in her mind over and over. She forced herself to make eye contact with her reflection.

"You're okay. They're okay," she whispered at her mirror image.

You're okay. They're okay, the image mouthed back at her.

Gradually, her panic eased. Her heartbeat slowed to normal, and her grip on the counter relaxed. Hollow and drained, she took several long, deep breaths, turned away from her reflection, and finished undressing.

You're okay. They're okay.

Back home, she would have tossed her clothes into a heap on the floor. Now, mindful that she had no others, she folded each damp item carefully and left them in a neat pile next to the sink. She retrieved her phone from her jeans pocket and set it next to the clothes along with the crumpled school letter. Then, shivering, she turned on the shower and stepped into the stall. The warm, soft spray cascaded over her aching muscles. She unwrapped a bar of soap and worked it to a lather in her hands. The sudsy water at her feet turned cloudy brown from the dirt and dust that had coated her skin and hair, then ran clear.

Five minutes later, shampooed, scrubbed clean, and wearing the oversize T-shirt and boxers, she returned to the sitting room. Her mother was standing outside on the tiny balcony, her arms crossed tightly over her body. It was freezing out there. Amazing what a giant temperature shift had occurred from just six hours before the tornado. That temperature gradient was a huge fueling factor for the tornado; Helicity knew it, but had never felt it.

Helicity hugged her mom hard from behind. "Mom?" she whispered. "Which bed should I sleep in?" She hoped her mother would let her sleep in the big bed with her, not by herself in the sofa bed.

Mrs. Dunlap turned into her embrace and stroked her damp hair. "I was thinking you and I could take the king, let your dad have the pullout if he comes tonight. Would you mind?"

Helicity burrowed in closer. "I don't mind," she murmured. "Not one bit."

". . . resulted in the deaths of six people, including a family of five, and widespread destruction to the town itself."

Nine o'clock the next morning, Helicity padded into the sitting room to find her mother watching the local news and sipping coffee from a paper cup. A half-eaten bagel and empty container of yogurt were on the table in front of her. The pullout was folded back into a sofa. It seemed her father had come sometime last night. If so, he'd already left.

"Hey, baby girl," her mother said. "I got you some juice and food for breakfast. It's all in the fridge."

Helicity latched on to something the newscaster had said. "Did anyone we know die?"

A look of anguish crossed Mrs. Dunlap's face. "We didn't know the family. Their children were much younger. Three-year-old twin girls and—and a little baby boy." She blinked rapidly, then shook her head. "The other person was an older woman who lived alone on the outskirts of town. Again . . . no one we knew."

Helicity breathed a sigh of relief, then felt guilty for being relieved. That woman, whoever she was, must have had people who cared about her. Now she was gone from their lives forever. And a whole family . . . Her mind seized up and refused to go there. It was just too horrifying to think about.

Instead, she found her breakfast and returned to sit next to her mother. Live video of her ruined town was playing on the television. Huge waste-removal trucks, heavy-duty construction equipment, and emergency vehicles drove around and through the wreckage. Men and women in hard hats and fluorescent-colored clothing walked about the destroyed buildings, snapping photos, taking notes on clipboards, and tapping on handheld tablets. Recovery dogs accompanied the Task Force of Michigan, marking each home and car with a different color neon *X*—a code allowing them to quickly communicate the fate of whoever had been inside. The whole scene seemed unreal to Helicity, like computer-generated clips for a natural-disaster movie.

If only that's what they were, she thought as she drank her apple juice.

"Cleanup efforts have begun," the announcer reported, "but more volunteers are needed to assist in removing the enormous piles of debris." Helicity found the matter-of-factness the anchor spoke in to be annoying and trivializing. She continued, "If you cannot volunteer but would like to help those displaced by the tornado, please consider donating to one of the following disaster-relief organizations." A list of names and contact information appeared on the screen.

"One final request," the broadcaster added. She tapped her papers into a neat stack and then looked solemnly into the camera. "Many people assume they should send goods directly to the affected community. Your generosity is greatly appreciated, but you are urged to give money rather than personal items. Delivering, opening, and sorting through individual packages is very costly and time-consuming, and too often, the items sent are not what is needed most by the victims."

Victims, Helicity repeated to herself. *Is that what we are?* She supposed it was true. Yet the label bothered her. It made her feel helpless and out of control. She hadn't liked that feeling when it hit her in the bathroom the night before, and she liked the idea of being categorized that way even less now.

"That's enough news for this morning." Mrs. Dunlap hit the Off button on the remote, and the television screen turned black.

"Where's Dad?" Helicity asked. She assumed he'd returned to Andy's side, but after seeing the trucks on TV, she wondered if he'd gone to assist with the cleanup and rebuilding instead.

"Gone to the hospital already." Mrs. Dunlap got up and poured the remains of her coffee down the sink. "The hotel helped us get rental cars. He took one, and we'll head over in the other once you're ready."

Helicity looked down at her T-shirt and boxers. "Um . . ."

Mrs. Dunlap flickered a brief smile. "Don't worry. The hotel has a laundry facility in the basement, thank God. Your clothes are clean and in the bathroom. After we see Andy, we'll stop at the store and pick up some other things."

The next hours passed in a blur. At the hospital, her father gave her a cursory hug, but it held little warmth, giving her the clear message that he was still upset with her. She sat with Andy for a short time while her parents talked with the doctor outside the room. Andy was so groggy from painkillers, he didn't do much more than smile and mumble, "Hey, Hel," before dozing off. As she watched him sleep, she felt an unexpected emotion: anger.

Why'd you have to come after me? I'm not a baby. I can take care of myself!

Mrs. Dunlap came into the room then. Mistaking her daughter's scowl for concern, she said, "Hey, hon, don't worry about Andy. Rest is the best thing for him right now."

Helicity's anger melted into shame. Her throat tightened. What right did she have to be mad at Andy? She knew why he'd come after her—because he was her big brother and he loved her.

She and her mother left Mr. Dunlap at the hospital with Andy and went to a nearby department store. They filled a shopping cart with basic clothing items, inexpensive shoes, toiletries, food, water, and other essentials, including cell phone chargers.

Another wave of shame washed over Helicity when she saw those last items. Her mother nudged her with her shoulder. "You can't change what happened," she said with a nod toward the chargers, "but you can learn from it. Right?"

"Right," Helicity mumbled.

At the register, a bored checkout girl asked if they

wanted to donate to the store's Tornado Victims Aid Fund.

Victims, Helicity thought with another sudden flare of anger. There's that stupid word again.

"Thank you, no," Helicity's mother replied. "We're two of those victims."

The girl's head jerked up. Her mouth formed an O. "Jeez, I'm so sorry. I didn't— I hope you're okay. Really."

Her words were sympathetic, but her darting gaze was openly curious. Helicity beetled her brows and glared at her. The girl reddened and moved to the end of the checkout area. "Um, here, let me get your bags for you," she offered.

"I can do it," Helicity retorted. "I'm not helpless." She grabbed their purchases, dropped them in the cart, and pushed the cart out of the store.

"Slow down, Hel!" Her mother caught up to her in the parking lot and looked at her with concern. "Everything okay, baby girl?"

"I'm not a baby!"

The words shot out of Helicity's mouth before she

could stop them. Mrs. Dunlap's eyes widened with surprise. Helicity bit her lip and scuffed her feet on the pavement. "I'm sorry. I'm just . . . tired."

"Me, too, ba—hon. Me, too."

They made one last stop to pick up Mrs. Dunlap's laptop from her office at the community college where she worked. Back at the hotel, Helicity took one of the new cell phone chargers to the bedroom. She found an outlet and plugged in her phone. She dreaded seeing Andy's frantic message—*W R U???*—reappear when the phone came back to life.

But a lengthy chain of group texts from her classmates had long since crowded out Andy's message. As she scrolled through them, a frown slowly creased the space between her eyebrows. Some of her classmates had been away for the holiday weekend when the tornado hit. Unbelievably, a few of their texts were tinged with envy, as if they were sorry to have missed the storm. Other messages were nothing more than self-centered speculation about how the disaster would affect them.

One boy groused. A girl complained about the only ice cream parlor in town being gone. Another joked about going hunting for buried treasure in the wreckage.

> Something exciting finally happens to our town, and I'm not there!

Shaking her head with disbelief, Helicity clicked away from the text string. Her thoughts turned to Raven. She knew she couldn't ask her parents to take her looking for him. But she could at least get word out that he was missing. She clicked to the Facebook page that was set up for "victims" and posted a recent photo of her horse along with a plea for any information of his whereabouts. It wasn't much, but for the moment, it was the best she could do.

She was about to put her phone aside when she saw a message she'd missed from her best friend, Mia, earlier that morning.

> Hel, where are you?! Text me back the second you get this!

Helicity quickly typed a reply.
Mia answered immediately.

> Thank God you're okay! I heard about your house and Andy. I was freaking out when I didn't hear from you! How are you feeling?

Helicity pondered that last question. How was she feeling? Last night, the answer would have been anxious, exhausted, guilt-ridden, and out of control.

She still felt all those things, but now anger had been added to the mix. *Why anger, though?* she wondered. *I have no reason—no right—to be angry.*

In the end, she texted Mia the truth, that she was mostly feeling confused and tired. Then she lay back on the bed and closed her eyes to think about it some more.

Her phone buzzed. She assumed it was Mia replying and so was surprised to see a message from Andy instead.

> Sorry I conked out on you earlier! I'm awake and really bored. Call if you can.

With a happy smile, Helicity texted Mia she had to go so she could talk to Andy. Andy picked up on the first ring. "Hey, Hel! I was hoping you'd buzz."

"How are you doing?"

"Not going to lie," he replied. "My arm is killing me. The meds I'm on help. They're kind of fun, actually. Make me all loopy and then sleepy. As you saw for yourself earlier. I'll tell you the worst thing, though." He heaved an exaggerated sigh of disappointment. "All the nurses are old and not cute. Even the guys. Not a sexy one in the bunch."

Helicity giggled, relieved and delighted her brother sounded so much like himself. At his prodding, she spilled the story of what had happened to her after she left their parents' party. She didn't leave out anything—except that their father was furious with her and blamed her for the accident. But Andy had guessed that part anyway.

"I know what you're thinking, Hel," he said. "But Dad's not pointing fingers at you. At least, he hasn't said anything like that to me. And even if he does sorta kinda blame you right now, he'll get over it because he loves you." He gave a little laugh that turned into a cough. "He just doesn't get you sometimes," he finally managed to say.

"You mean because I'm not a guy, and I think weather is way more interesting than sports?" Helicity gave a short snort. "Yeah, tell me something I don't know."

"Actually, I'll tell you something you probably *do*

know, which is he'll come around a whole lot sooner if you make yourself useful. You know how he likes to see us helping out."

Helicity grunted her agreement because it was good advice. She didn't have a clue what she could do while they were in the hotel, though. She was about to say as much when Andy changed the subject.

"So. You saw it."

Helicity didn't understand what he meant at first. Then she realized *it* was the tornado. She pulled in her knees and fiddled with the end of her braid. "Yeah, I did."

"And?" he prompted. "I know what it was like close up—I don't recommend the experience, by the way— but what was it like seeing it from the hill?"

She closed her eyes and imagined herself back on the hilltop, looking down at the gathering storm below. "It was beautiful and terrifying and fascinating and incredible at first. I could see its strength and power, Andy. When the lightning lit up the sky and the clouds started whirling and changing, I thought . . . I felt . . . something inside me just . . ." She blew out an exasperated breath. "I can't describe it."

Andy chuckled. "You don't have to, Hel. Your voice says it all. Besides, been there, felt that. I know it's not exactly the same thing, but the first time I threw a touchdown pass, I got this amazing surge of emotion. Joy, I guess you'd call it, though that sounds kind of hokey coming from a big, strong dude like me."

Helicity laughed, but inside, she was squirming.

Joy. Had his injuries robbed him of the chance to throw those passes and feel that again?

Once more, he read her thoughts. "Hey, listen. The doctor said I'm doing great. I'll start rehab soon." His tone turned jaunty and joking. "Being the fine specimen of manly muscular health that I am, I'll be back on the field in no time."

"Really?" She desperately wanted to believe him.

"Totally. I'm a survivor, Hel." He gave a huge yawn into the phone then. "Phew, the pain meds are kicking in. Probably why I got all heavy, deep, and real just now. I gotta take another nap. But seriously, don't worry about me. I'll be fine."

"Okay. I'm coming to visit you tomorrow." They clicked off.

She put her phone aside, stretched out on the bed,

and replayed their conversation. One sentence in particular took hold in her mind.

I'm a survivor, Hel.

Survivor. That word resonated with her. It was so different in feel from *victim.* *Victim* made her think of defenseless people under attack, suffering helplessly. Weakened. In need of rescue.

Survivor, though . . . that had strength. It conjured up images of someone fighting back, overcoming odds, moving forward, persisting and succeeding in spite of huge obstacles. Someone like Andy.

She rolled over and curled into a ball. *And maybe someone like me?*

CHAPTER SEVEN

She must have dozed off because the next thing she knew, her mother was shaking her awake.

"Hey, kiddo. Sorry to get you up, but we have to get going in a few minutes."

Helicity sat up and rubbed her eyes. Outside the window, the sun had dipped low in the sky. "Going? Where?"

"They're holding a meeting about tornado relief at the community college. We need to be there."

Helicity got up. "I'll get ready."

Her mother blew out a breath. "We'll find out how to get help, what we need to do to start rebuilding, where we might live during rebuilding, that sort of thing."

"What about Dad?"

"He's returning his rental car and getting one of the company pickup trucks. He'll meet us there."

The community college theater where the meeting was being held was filling up fast when they arrived. The stage was set with a long table with microphones and chairs and an oversize screen. Someone was fiddling with a computer, trying to get it to connect to the screen. A few people cheered when the link finally worked.

Helicity scanned the crowd and spotted a petite girl with short coal-black hair and a heart-shaped face with a slightly upturned nose. "Mom, it's Mia! Can I go see her?"

Her mother nodded, and Helicity made her way to her friend. Mia's face lit up when she saw her. They hugged hard.

"Oh my gosh, Hel, you don't know how happy I was when I got your text! When I heard about Andy and your house . . ." Mia shook her head in shocked disbelief. "You need anything—and I mean anything, books, clothes, hair stuff, I don't even know what else but it doesn't even matter because if I've got it, it's yours. You just let me know. In the meantime, here." She shoved a package in Helicity's hands. "It's just a notebook and a bunch of colored pens. I brought them in case I saw you here. I thought you might want to write out some of your feelings." She shrugged. "It's what I do to get through the tough stuff. So trust me. It helps."

Mia's parents had gone through a messy divorce a year earlier. An only child, Mia still got caught in the middle of their heated battles.

Helicity's eyes welled at her friend's thoughtfulness. "You didn't have to do that!"

Mia waved her hands as if erasing the sentence from the air. "And you didn't have to listen to me go on and on about my parents all last year. You, my therapist, and a shelf-load of these babies"—she tapped the package—"got me through a freaking nightmare. About time I returned the favor, Hel."

Helicity hugged Mia again. "Listen, I'm going to

sit with my mom, but I'll look for you after, okay? And, Mia?" She smoothed her hand over the present. "Thanks."

The meeting began shortly after Helicity took her seat. First to speak was the school superintendent, who informed the audience that the remaining two weeks of school would be held here, at the community college, starting the next day. Students were strongly encouraged to attend.

Immediately after this announcement, Helicity's phone buzzed. She peeked at the text and had to shove a hand in her mouth to suppress a giggle. Mia had reacted to the superintendent's news by sending an emoji with its tongue out and eyes crossed. When her mother looked at her questioningly, she showed her what Mia had sent. Her mother smiled—her first real smile since the tornado. Seeing it loosened something tight inside Helicity's chest. She smiled back, sent a laughing emoji to Mia, and returned the phone to her pocket.

The presentations turned to matters of insurance, personal finance, and other adult-oriented top-ics. Helicity tried to follow along, but soon gave up.

Midway through, her father, looking worn-out and reeking of stale cigarettes, slipped into the seat next to her mother. When he caught Helicity looking at him, he frowned and jerked his head toward the stage, a clear message that he expected her to pay attention. She clutched Mia's present and kept her eyes forward after that.

The meeting concluded a short while later with the main speaker urging attendees to consult the disaster relief and recovery website that had been set up for their town. "It's your best first step to getting answers," she said.

As the audience began gathering their belongings, a young woman burst through the back doors. "Excuse me!" she called as she hurried to the stage. "If I could have your attention for just one more minute?"

People stopped talking and turned to look at her. She was tall and slender with sun-kissed skin and long, curly blond hair tied back in a low, loose ponytail. She wore faded jeans and a pale green scoop-necked jersey under a denim jacket. A long necklace with a lightning bolt–shaped pendant hung around her neck. Dangling earrings winked from beneath wispy curls that had strayed from the ponytail. She moved to center stage, her low-heeled boots rapping a staccato on the wood floor, and freed a microphone from its holder.

"Hi," she said. The microphone gave a shrill screech. She made a face and turned it off, trusting her booming voice instead. "My name is Lana McElvoy. I'm a meteorologist. I teach science courses here at the college. I'm hoping someone out there took pictures or video of the tornado. Because if you did, I sure would like to see them."

A long silence greeted Lana McElvoy's request. Then a man stepped into the aisle and shouted, "Lady, you got some nerve."

She held up her hands. "Sir, I understand—"

"No, I don't think you do." The man stalked to the front of the stage and glared up at her. "A tornado ripped through our town not twenty-four hours ago. People are hurt. Seven are dead." The fury in his voice echoed throughout the theater. "If someone stopped to film this disaster instead of helping"—he looked out over the audience with narrowed eyes—"then that person has a whole lot of explaining to do, if you ask me."

"You got that right, Foster!" Mr. Dunlap said loudly. "And if someone did film it, he better not post it on social media. I mean, my God. How can you call it *social* when you stand back and record instead of reaching out to help someone in trouble?"

People around Helicity murmured their agreement. They turned away from the woman onstage and began filing into the aisles.

"Wait, please!" Lana pleaded. "I apologize if my request seemed insensitive. Please know you all have my greatest sympathy. And I don't want to do anything to add to your troubles. Quite the opposite." She moved to the edge of the stage and held her arms out wide, as if to encompass them all. "My goal is to gather information about the storm. What the sky looked like beforehand. The storm's overall behavior. I want to learn from this tragedy so I can work to prevent other communities from going through what you're facing. If anyone is willing to talk to me about what they witnessed, what they experienced . . ."

Her voice trailed off as people turned a deaf ear to

her and continued to depart. She shook her head. "I'll be happy to provide you with my contact information," she finished with a disappointed sigh.

Mr. Dunlap shook his head, then spun on his heel and jerked his head at Helicity and her mother. "Let's go," he growled to them. Mrs. Dunlap followed behind her husband.

Helicity moved that way, too, but much more slowly.

Her hand stole to her back pocket, touching her phone. Captured in its memory were exactly the kinds of visuals the meteorologist was looking for. Lana McElvoy's reason for wanting such images made total sense to her. She knew from watching programs and reading books about weather-forecasting that studying all aspects of devastating storms help scientists understand them better. Eyewitness accounts and footage are critical to completing the overall picture. The more the scientists understand, the earlier they can recognize the warning signs of an impending natural disaster. Early detection leads to earlier alerts, and earlier alerts save lives.

How many more people might have perished

yesterday without the town siren and the phone notifications? Helicity wondered.

Still, she was hesitant to share what her phone held in its memory.

Dad's already angry with me. If he finds out I was taking pictures and video, and that that's why my battery died, I'm dead. Plus, it's pretty clear he doesn't appreciate what Lana McElvoy's trying to do.

She understood his anger. There were people out there these days who seemed to take great delight in trivializing, even mocking, horrific tragedies—as the group texts she'd read from her classmates that morning proved. Because of people like that, she had no intention of posting her material online. And yet, if she didn't reach out to Lana, she'd always wonder if her video, photos, and observations might have been helpful. If even one person could benefit from what was stored on her phone . . .

She risked a glance over her shoulder. Lana had made her way offstage and was coming up the aisle toward her. Helicity's heartbeat quickened. If she was going to act, now was the moment.

I'm going to do it.

Thinking fast, she let Mia's gift slip from her grasp. "Whoops!" She squatted to pick it up, blocking the aisle as she did.

Lana gave Helicity a polite smile and then moved to pass her.

"Wait!" Helicity whispered. "I—I have some." Her urgency must have rung true because Lana hesitated and began patting the pockets of her jacket as if she was checking for something.

"Some what?" she whispered to Helicity.

"Photos. Video. On my phone. But my dad—"

"Hel! Let's go!"

Mr. Dunlap's sharp call brought Helicity to her feet instantly. Her back to her father, her eyes met Lana's, pleading with her not to say anything.

Lana winked her understanding. Then she pushed past Helicity, purposefully bumping her off-balance as she did. When Helicity stumbled, Lana grabbed her by the hand. "I'm so sorry!" she apologized.

"That's okay," Helicity said. But Lana was already making her way up the aisle. She brushed by Mr. Dunlap without a glance. He turned to stare after her, which gave Helicity the chance to peek at the business card Lana had pressed into her palm.

Lana McElvoy, Meteorologist and Storm Chaser, it read. Below were phone numbers, a website, social media information, and an e-mail address.

"Helicity!" her father called impatiently.

"Coming, Dad! Sorry!"

She quickly slipped the card in her pocket and hurried out of the theater.

CHAPTER EIGHT

Helicity emerged from the theater and looked for Mia in the lobby. Instead, she found herself face-to-face with Pete. He was wearing his civilian clothes, not his police uniform, so she didn't recognize him until he spoke.

"I hoped I'd see you here," he said. "I think I found something of yours." He pulled out his phone and showed her a photo.

Helicity gasped. "That's Raven! You found him! Where is he? Is he safe? Can I see him?"

Pete grinned. "He's fine. A farmer spotted him this morning wandering on the outskirts of town. She keeps a few horses herself, so she took him in, put him in a free stall where he's been happy as a clam ever since. I would have let you know sooner, but I didn't know how to reach you."

He handed her a slip of paper. "Here's the farmer's address and contact info. For the record, she seems very nice. Maybe you can work something out with her for Raven to stay there if . . . well, you know."

Helicity nodded her understanding. Raven's barn, like so many other buildings, had been destroyed by the tornado. Her horse was as homeless as she, her parents, and so many of their neighbors were.

Helicity thanked Pete over and over, then hurried off, hoping to catch Mia. But her mother told her they had to get going. "Dad and I have a lot to figure out," she said.

Her father had left for the hotel in the company pickup truck already. In the car, Helicity told her mother what she'd learned about Raven, including Pete's suggestion to ask if they could stable him there. "Oh, honey, that's great news. I'm sure we can make it work," her mother reassured her.

They picked up dinner at a fast-food drive-through,

then continued on to the Lakeside. In their room, her father ate his burger and fries at the kitchen countertop while hunkered over his wife's laptop. Eyes darting, he scanned the disaster relief and recovery website they'd learned about at the meeting. Helicity's mother sat next to him, picking at her salad and leaning in awkwardly to get a better view of the screen.

Helicity knew not to ask her father about Raven just then. She took her food into the bedroom and left the door ajar, turned on the television, and ate her dinner while watching a show.

The whole time, the meteorologist's card burned a hole in her pocket.

When she was finished eating, she went into the bathroom, locked the door, and took out the card and her phone. She thumbed to her photo cache and pulled up the first image she'd taken of the brewing storm. With quick flicks of her fingertip, she swiped through one after another. Then she opened the first video.

". . . is about to get walloped." Her recorded voice echoed off the tiles in the bathroom. She hurriedly decreased the volume, then watched with fascination as the storm unfolded on the tiny screen. Helicity watched the second video, too. She heard herself say, "Raven, I think we'd better—" Then the picture jerked violently, marking the moment the tornado alert had blared and she'd dropped the phone.

Aside from that abrupt ending, the video itself looked as good as any Helicity had seen of storms. So did the photos. They captured the dramatic transformation playing out on the horizon: the cloud movement, flashes of lightning, the thickening wall cloud, the darkening green-black sky.

She turned Lana's business card around in her hand. *I could just send one to her. A few quick taps on the screen is all it would take. Then I could throw away her card and that would be the end of it.*

Except . . . she didn't want it to end there.

Meteorologist and Storm Chaser. Those job titles reached out and grabbed Helicity. She'd always been drawn to the weather—its power, its changeable nature, its beauty and fury. To her, it was a living, breathing entity. As a young child, she'd pictured it as having moods: warm and sunny, gray and gloomy, cold and aloof, rainy and sad, windy and playful. As she grew older, she became interested in the atmospheric forces that caused those moods to change. Wind, moisture, pressure, temperature—there was so much about the weather that she didn't know, and so much she wanted to understand.

The atmosphere was a puzzle she needed to solve. In fact, that desire to understand was the reason she'd even considered bumping up to the honors-level science and math classes. A solid grasp of both subjects was critical to understanding and forecasting the weather. Even though she was only thirteen—soon to be fourteen—she didn't want to risk falling behind. Not if she could prevent it.

Meteorologist and Storm Chaser. The first was Helicity's secret dream career. As for the second, she'd viewed hundreds of clips of shaky, rain-spattered video taken from dashboard and handheld cams by storm chasers racing into the teeth of extreme weather phenomena. The fierce winds, driving rain, snow, and hail that blasted the vehicles sometimes drowned out the audio. But the chasers' exhilaration, awe, and raw fear still came through loud and clear, leaving Helicity with the strong impression that pursuing storms, especially tornadoes, was very important, potentially dangerous, and absolutely thrilling.

And now she'd met a woman who did both things she longed to do. She traced her finger over Lana's name and thought back to their encounter in the auditorium. As brief as it had been, she'd felt a connection spark between them. The meteorologist had come across as confident, strong, and intelligent. She could easily imagine Lana shouting instructions to a driver, urging him or her to get them even closer to a raging tempest.

Man, how awesome would it be to hear about her experiences? To pick her brain? To learn from her?

Contact her, an inner voice encouraged her, *before this chance slips away!*

But another voice rang out just as loudly. *Destroy the card. Delete the photos and video before your father finds out,* it warned sternly.

She stared at herself in the mirror. "Hey," she whispers after a long moment. "You are not a victim. You are a survivor. Take control of what happens next." She brushed a lock of hair away from her forehead and lifted her chin. "Or do you want to be a survivor who takes charge of what happens next?"

Helicity made up her mind. She chose the best storm photo and, thumbs flying over the phone's tiny touchpad, typed a text.

> Hi, Ms. McElvoy. It's me, the girl from the auditorium. Here's a photo I took of the storm. I don't know if it's any good, but I have others if you want to see them. There's 2 videos, too. Tx. Helicity Dunlap

She hit Send before she could change her mind. Then she sagged against the bathroom counter.

Well, she thought. That's that. Either Lana McElvoy would respond or she wouldn't. And either her father would find out and be even more furious with her, or he wouldn't.

Andy's advice to make herself useful popped into her head then. She pocketed her phone and Lana's card and went into the sitting room, intending to ask her parents if there was anything she could do for them. But the perfect idea came to her when she spied the shopping bags of clothes still on the sofa. She dumped the contents onto the table, retrieved a steak knife from the kitchen, and began cutting off sales tags.

Her parents looked up from the laptop. "What are you doing, hon?" her mother asked, perplexed.

"You guys are really busy, so I thought I'd do our laundry," Helicity replied, unearthing a small bottle of detergent from another bag. "Would that be okay?"

Mrs. Dunlap blinked in surprise. "That'd be great, actually. Thank you."

Helicity's father raised his eyebrows, then nodded approvingly. He pulled out his wallet and removed some money along with one of the room keys. "You'll need cash for the laundry. Oh, and I saw some vending machines by the elevator. Get us all some M&M'S on your way back up, why don't you, kiddo. No peanut ones, now! You know how I feel about them!" He winked at her.

As she took the money and key, Helicity sent Andy a silent thank-you for his advice. Then she said in an ultra-serious voice, "Only peanut ones. Got it." Her joke earned her a smile from her father. She bagged the laundry, headed out the door, and rode the elevator to the basement floor.

She'd only done laundry a few times in her life, but fortunately, instructions for using the machines were posted on the wall. She'd just stuffed the first loads into the washers when her phone buzzed, alerting her that she had an incoming text.

Lana? Her stomach flip-flopped. But the text was from Mia, asking her to call if she could. Helicity dialed her number right away.

Mia launched into the conversation without so much as a hello. "Please tell me you'll be there tomorrow!"

"Be where?" Helicity asked.

"School at the community college, remember?" Mia replied. "I need to know someone else is going!"

Helicity had forgotten about school. "I'm sure I will be," she said. "My mom might have some work stuff to do at the college anyway."

"Okay, good. Do you need me to bring you anything—clothes, shoes, whatever?"

Helicity smiled, imagining her lankier frame squeezed into Mia's petite-size shirts and even smaller sneakers. "No, I'm all set for the next few days. Mom and I shopped earlier, and now I'm doing the laundry."

"Laundry? You? Wow. Impressive."

They talked a while longer, then Helicity heard voices in the background on Mia's end. Mia sighed.

"That's my grandmother calling. She wants me to walk her dog. I'll see you tomorrow."

Mia hung up after getting Helicity to promise to meet her on the front steps of the community college's main building the next morning. An instant later, Helicity's phone rang. Assuming it was Mia calling about something she'd forgotten to say, she answered with a tone of fake exasperation. "*Now* what do you want?"

Silence greeted her. Then a woman asked, "This is Lana McElvoy. May I speak to Helicity Dunlap?"

Helicity gulped. "Ms. McElvoy!" she stammered with embarrassment. "I'm so sorry! I thought you were my friend Mia! I—"

Lana chuckled. It was a soothing sound. "Oh, no worries! And please, call me Lana. Now, before I ask you anything else, I have to know: Is your name really Helicity? Or were you just trying to get my attention by using that term?"

"No," Helicity said, "that's my name. I got it in honor of my grandmother, Doris Picossi."

"Doris Picossi?" Lana echoed. "You don't mean Doris Picossi, the physicist, do you?"

"Um, yeah, that's her. She was my mom's mother."

"No way!" Lana sounded impressed. "I've read some of her work. She was brilliant! Do you mind if I ask what she was like?"

"I wish I could tell you," Helicity replied with regret. "But she died just before I was born."

"Ah." Lana was quiet, and then she asked Helicity how she and her family were doing, where they were staying, and other similar questions. After Helicity answered them all, Lana said, "So tell me, Helicity Dunlap, how long have you been a weather junkie?"

"How'd you know?" Helicity asked, surprised.

"You know that expression 'It takes one to know one'?" Lana said. "Well, I'm one, so I recognized you as one. And I've met a few like us in my travels. Maybe someday I'll introduce you to them. In the meantime, about that photo you sent—"

Helicity held her breath.

"—it was a fantastic image. I'd love to see what else you've got."

"Really?" Helicity's voice came out as a high-pitched squeak of delight.

Lana chuckled again. "Absolutely. I heard your school is holding classes at the community college. I have an office there. Think you can squeeze some time out of your day tomorrow to visit me so I can meet the granddaughter of Doris Picossi and see her other pics?"

"I sure—"

"Who are you talking to?"

Helicity whirled around to find her father standing in the laundry room doorway. They locked eyes.

"Hello? Helicity? You there?" Lana asked.

"Um, yeah," Helicity answered, still held in the grip of her father's stare. "But I have to go."

"Oh, okay. See you tomorrow, though, right?"

Helicity hung up without replying.

"So." Mr. Dunlap leaned on the doorjamb and narrowed his eyes. "Care to tell me who that was?"

CHAPTER NINE

"I was talking with Mia," Helicity blurted. It wasn't a lie, exactly—she had been talking to Mia earlier. "We were making plans to meet tomorrow. You know, for classes."

Her father regarded her for another second, then pushed off the door and peered at the washing machine control panels. "Looks like these have a ways to go. In the meantime, did you take care of that other errand yet?"

"Other . . . ?"

"Don't tell me you forgot." Mr. Dunlap crossed his arms. "M&M'S, remember?"

Relief flooded Helicity's body. "Right! I was about to get them when my phone rang."

Luckily, her father didn't probe any further. If he had, Helicity suspected she would have cracked and told him all about her contact with Lana McElvoy.

"Come on." Mr. Dunlap smiled. "We'll get 'em together. Eat all the good ones before your mom can get her hands on them."

"You know they all taste the same, right?"

Her father snorted. "Who told you that lie?"

Helicity slept on the pullout that night. In the morning, she put on one of her newly washed outfits and rode to the community college with her mother.

"Come to the office when you're done," Mrs. Dunlap said as they went their separate ways. "Oh, and by the way, I'll contact that farmer today. Maybe later we can go see Raven."

Helicity nodded happily and then left. She was very familiar with the campus and made her way straight to the front steps. Mia was waiting. They joined other sixth-, seventh-, and eighth-grade students in the same auditorium where the previous night's meeting had been held. By Helicity's reckoning, nearly one-third of the middle school student body was absent. Many who were there were surreptitiously using their cell phones. Under normal circumstances, students weren't allowed to have phones with them during school time. But these were far from normal circumstances. Helicity had overheard more than one classmate say their parents wouldn't have let them come if they couldn't keep their phones with them at all times.

As for those students who weren't there, she assumed they had their reasons for not attending. For her part, she couldn't wait to get out of the hotel room that morning, even though it meant going to school. As nice as their accommodations were, after two days the walls were starting to close in on her—and the occasional waves of tension between her parents were stressing her out.

Not that they'd be staying there much longer. Using his connections in the construction and real estate business, her father had found them a furnished three-bedroom house to rent for the summer while their own home was being rebuilt. She and her parents would move there on Saturday. Hopefully, Andy would be strong enough by then to join them.

"Good morning, students." Ms. Stockwell, the middle school principal, stood in front of the stage. "Thank you for coming. As you know, there were two weeks remaining in the school year before the—the tragedy hit our town. The middle school was badly damaged, so having classes there was impossible. Fortunately, the community college has opened its doors to us."

A student sitting in back stage-whispered a sarcastic comment about how unfortunate that was. Ms. Stockwell ignored him.

"We will not be holding classes as such," she continued. "Instead, we will have study sessions to prepare you for end-of-term exams, which will be given the latter part of next week. In addition"—her voice turned somber—"we will be holding group counseling sessions to help you process what has happened to our community. We encourage you to sign up for at least one, if not more. Now, please find your homeroom teacher. He or she will bring you to your assigned classroom. Thank you."

Helicity and Mia followed their homeroom teacher,

Mr. Albright, to a lecture room. They were in all the same classes, so for the next few hours, they worked together creating study guides and review sheets for their upcoming exams.

Helicity did her best to focus, but a good chunk of her mind was wondering when she might meet up with Lana. She found out when Mr. Albright announced a one-hour break for lunch, adding that classes would conclude around two thirty. While other kids moved toward the college's dining hall, Helicity sent Lana a message.

> Hi, Lana! I should be done with school by 2:30. Can I come by then?

Lana's reply came a moment later.

> Yes! My office is open. It's room 380. If I'm not there, just go on in.

"Hey, Hel, you coming?" Mia called. "I heard Tater Tots are on the menu."

Helicity put her phone away and joined Mia. She was grinning from ear to ear.

"Okay, what's with the big smile?" Mia asked. "It can't be the Tater Tots."

"What? Oh, no, it's not the tots." Helicity quickly filled Mia in on her upcoming meeting.

Mia gave a low whistle. "You're going to meet a woman who does exactly what you want to do when you're all grown up? How cool is that?"

"I know! Hey, you want to come with me? I bet she wouldn't mind."

Mia shook her head regretfully. "Can't. Mom's picking me up at two thirty sharp. But call me after and tell me all about it!"

Two and a half hours later, Helicity stood in front of Lana McElvoy's office. The door was ajar. She gave a tentative knock, then pushed it open when no one answered.

"Whoa."

The office space was just big enough for a file cabinet, two chairs, and a desk with a widescreen computer and a neglected-looking ivy plant. On the wall behind the desk was an oversize bulletin board. Tacked to it were menus from local restaurants, tiny slips of paper from fortune cookies, a list labeled *Emergency Contacts*, and a yellowed newspaper clipping with the headline STORM CHASER CHEATS DEATH. There were also photographs of men and women posing at the back of a bizarre-looking vehicle stocked with electronics and weather equipment. Helicity recognized a younger Lana McElvoy in several of the photos.

But it was the framed artwork covering the wall opposite the desk that really took her breath away.

One section held spectacular photographs of different storms. Dusty-brown, sooty-black, and dishwater-gray tornadoes shaped like thick columns, thin twisted curves, and wide-mouthed cones. Vast hurricanes captured by orbiting satellites, the storms' circular eyes staring blankly up into space. Trees and street signs bent to the ground by violent winds. Drenching rains flooding city streets and rural pastures. One particularly arresting image was of a "mother ship"—a supercell thunderstorm of dense, layered clouds shaped like a squat cylinder—that hovered malevolently over an isolated farmhouse. What made it so fascinating was the sun-drenched blue sky peeking around it.

Helicity's gaze traveled to the next section of images. These weren't pictures of storms, but posters of movies that featured storms. *The Wizard of Oz*, with its famous house-whirling tornado, hung between the disaster films *The Day After Tomorrow*, about a superstorm that instantly plunges New York City into a deadly ice age, and *The Perfect Storm*, a true story about fishermen who underestimate the storms that hit their boat and consequently all die. When Helicity saw the next group of posters, she laughed aloud. They were for the Sharknado movies, absurd but hugely popular cult hits about massive tornadoes and waterspouts (basically tornadoes that occur over water)—that suck up and deposit deadly sharks in the storm-flooded streets of various major US cities.

Still chuckling, Helicity took a step back to get a better view of the wall as a whole. When she did, she bumped into the desk. The computer had been in sleep mode, but suddenly, the picture she'd sent Lana the night before materialized on the screen. She gasped.

Up until that moment, she'd only seen the photo on her phone's tiny screen. Now her jaw dropped at the details revealed by the much bigger image and higher resolution. She leaned forward, intending to use the computer touch screen to zero in even more.

"Hey! What do you think you're doing? Leave that alone!"

Helicity jumped back, startled by the sharp voice. She turned to find a teenage boy scowling at her. His ice-blue eyes were fierce and penetrating. Although he wasn't big—nowhere near Andy's size—he filled the doorway, blocking the only way out. His spiky black hair, retro T-shirt with heavy-metal band logo, ripped jeans, black leather wristbands, and thick-soled combat boots made him even more intimidating. A black leather jacket hung from his finger over his shoulder.

"What are you doing?" he demanded again, taking a step into the office.

Helicity shrank away from him. "Lana told me to— to meet her here," she stammered.

The boy took another step toward her. "And did Lana also tell you to mess around with her computer?"

Helicity shook her head. "I just wanted to see my photograph better," she mumbled. "I didn't mean to—"

"Wait." The boy's scowl vanished abruptly. "What do you mean, *your* photograph?"

Helicity pointed at the computer screen. "I took that picture."

The boy looked from the photo to Helicity and back. "You took that? Seriously?" He dragged his fingers through his hair, making it spike up even more. One corner of his mouth lifted in a mischievous half grin, and his icy glare melted. "Then that makes you Helicity Dunlap. Sorry. She told me she was meeting you today. I didn't know when. Also, I didn't know you were so young."

Helicity drew herself up. "I'm going to be fourteen this summer."

"That old, huh?" he said in a teasing but not unfriendly tone. "My name's Sam, by the way. I'm part of Lana's team. And for the record, I'll be eighteen next year." The boy's impish smile broadened, and a butterfly in Helicity's stomach suddenly took flight.

Footsteps rapped in the hallway. A second later, Lana hurried in with an armload of books. She beamed at Helicity. "You're here! Excellent!" She butted Sam with her hip. "Yo. Out of my way before my arms break."

Sam shifted next to Helicity. He smelled outdoorsy, like newly mown grass and tropical-scented sunscreen with a hint of campfire smoke. It was a nice smell, she thought, and her stomach butterfly fluttered again.

Lana deposited the books on her file cabinet. Then she flopped into her desk chair with a sigh of relief, laced her hands behind her head, and swiveled to regard them. "So, you two have met. Sam, what do you think of Helicity's camera work?"

"She captured a great image. It could be on your wall. People might even pay a decent amount of money for it," he answered, jerking his chin toward the framed photographs.

Helicity blushed. "Thanks," she said. "Do you want to see the others?"

"Yes," Lana and Sam replied simultaneously.

Helicity pulled out her phone. Several taps and the whooshing sound of a sent e-mail later, Lana's in-box pinged an incoming message alert.

"Ah, technology. How I love you," Lana murmured. She swiveled back around to face her computer and downloaded the attachments. She clicked over to her Pictures folder and opened the images as a page of thumbnails. Helicity and Sam moved to stand on either side of her to get a better look.

Laid out together in sequence, the first photos followed the storm's progress from billowing, sun-lit clouds to dark, angry wall in minute detail. The next showed the clear area beneath the clouds turning into a gray haze of rain as the storm intensified. The last picture captured the start of the spinning motion beneath the wall.

Lana's eyes shifted from one to the next. "Nice. Very nice." She pointed to the last one, glanced back at Helicity, and murmured, "Your namesake."

"You've got to send these to me, too," Sam added.

Helicity bit her lip and nodded. As with the single photo she had seen enlarged for the first time on Lana's computer, this was the first time she'd seen all her photos together on one page. Following their progression, she was suddenly catapulted back to the hilltop as the storm raged overhead. Her heart started pounding in her chest. She couldn't breathe. The images swam in front of her eyes, her knees buckled, and she collapsed.

CHAPTER TEN

"**W**hoa, whoa, whoa!" Sam yanked over the spare office chair and sat Helicity down in it. He knelt in front of her. "You okay there, Fourteen?"

Helicity squeezed her eyes shut tight. *I'm a survivor, not a victim. I'm a survivor, not a victim.* She repeated the words in her mind, willing them to take root in her brain.

Someone gently grasped her hands. "Helicity. Breathe deeply. In and out. Nice and slow."

It was Lana. She slid her hands to the insides of Helicity's wrists and pressed gently. "These are pressure points," she murmured. "Sometimes, a little push on them helps calm a troubled mind."

Lana's soft voice soothed Helicity; she thought the touch on her pressure points did, too. Slowly, she felt the panic ebb. She opened her eyes and found herself staring into Lana's deep brown ones.

"I'm okay." She pulled in another deep breath and let it out. Lana continued to hold her gaze and her wrists. "I'm a survivor, not a victim."

"Sam," Lana said quietly, "give us a minute, will you?"

"But—"

Lana looked up at him. "And close the door. Thanks."

Sam made a sound like he was about to protest but then thought better of it. He stood up and left without another word, pulling the door shut with a click behind him.

Lana turned to face Helicity again. Her expression was concerned. "I thought it might be easier for you to talk without Sam here."

"Talk?"

"About your experience."

Helicity glanced at the computer where her photos

were still laid out on the screen. Lana reached behind her and closed out the page. "Not what you saw," she murmured. "What you experienced, during and after the tornado. What you're experiencing now, in the wake of the storm. Talking about it might help you process everything just a little more."

Helicity nodded slowly. Then she told Lana everything. Her ride up the hilltop to think about high school. Her initial awe and then her growing alarm at seeing the gathering storm. Andy's accident and the possible end of his football prospects. Her father's fury and her own guilt. Finally, she revealed her hope of one day being just like Lana.

Throughout, Lana murmured comments—"That's how you got such amazing pictures"; "That's why your father was angry with my request last night"; and "That's why you reached out to me even though you risked making him angrier"—as if Helicity's story filled in some blanks for her.

When Helicity was done, Lana sat back and steepled her fingertips at her lips. "So this letter from school, the one that set your story in motion, did it give a deadline for overriding?"

"I've got it right here. Let me check." Helicity opened her notebook and pulled out the letter, now soft and wrinkled from handling. She smoothed it out and found the deadline. "It says I have until July 31. Why?"

Lana tilted her head to one side. "Can I ask what's holding you back?"

Helicity dug her toe into the floor. "My teachers don't think I can handle the work. I'm not sure my parents do, either, and I need their permission to bump up to the next level."

"Hey."

Helicity looked up and met Lana's gaze.

"Do *you* think you can handle it?" Lana asked.

Helicity chewed her bottom lip, thinking about the question. Finally, she shook her head. "I'm not sure," she answered honestly. "But I want to try. That won't change my parents' minds, though."

Lana nodded thoughtfully. "You have end-of-term exams next week, right? If you ace them, would that make your parents agree to sign off on the override, do you think?"

Helicity blinked. "Maybe. It would help, at least, that's for sure."

Lana rolled her chair over to the office door and opened it. "Sam, you still out there?" she called.

Sam stuck his head inside. "At your service. What's up?"

"You know how I said I'd keep an ear out for students for you to tutor?" Lana inclined her head at Helicity. "Found you one."

"Huh?" Helicity and Sam said at the same time.

Lana chuckled. "You've never tutored before, Sam. Before I send students your way, you need to prove you can do it. Helicity has final exams next week. You help her get the math and science material down cold so she passes with flying colors, and I'll see about finding you some students."

"But . . . don't tutors get paid? I don't have any money," Helicity said. "Or at least, not a lot."

Lana waved away her concern. "Sam wouldn't accept payment anyway. Would you, Sam?"

Sam heaved a huge sigh, pretending to be put out. "No, I suppose not. But I have one condition. You send me those photos!"

Helicity agreed readily, and when Sam rattled off his contact info, she entered it in her phone and then forwarded the images to him. He nodded his head with satisfaction when his phone pinged.

"Then it's settled," Lana said. "You can use my office at this time every afternoon, starting tomorrow. I'll sit in as often as I can to help out and observe Sam's teaching style. How's that sound?"

Sam and Helicity exchanged glances. Then Sam laughed. "We might as well say yes, Fourteen. Lana's got it all figured out anyway."

"In that case . . . yes. On one condition," Helicity said. Sam raised his eyebrows questioningly. "Stop calling me Fourteen."

Helicity left Lana's office soon after that and made her way to the Human Resources building, where her mother worked recruiting new instructors and other staff. Mrs. Dunlap greeted her with an exhausted smile. "I'll be just a few minutes," she promised.

"No problem," Helicity reassured her. Then, after a moment's hesitation, she added, "Hey, Mom, you know that woman from the meeting last night who works here, the meteorologist Lana McElvoy?"

"Mmm-hmmm," her mother responded distract-edly as she shuffled through some papers.

"Well, I just met her. She's really nice. In fact, I'm going to be—"

"Oh, shoot." Mrs. Dunlap interrupted with a groan of exasperation. "These aren't the right forms. Sorry, honey, you're going to have to wait a little longer so I can get this sorted out."

While her mother hurried to correct the paperwork issue, Helicity took a seat in the office easy chair and called Mia.

Mia answered on the first ring. "Hey, H, how'd it go with the weather woman?"

"Meteorologist," Helicity corrected. "Great, actually. There was this boy—"

"Ooooo!" Mia cooed. "There was, was there? Was he cute?"

Helicity felt herself blushing. "Cut it out, Mia. Sheesh. He was almost as old as Andy!"

"So?"

"So . . . he's going to be tutoring me after school this week and next."

"Tutoring you? Why?" Mia wanted to know.

"Well, I want to do really well on the exams. Math and science in particular."

"Why?" Mia asked again.

"Because I'm thinking about going up to the honors levels in those courses next year."

Mia didn't reply.

"Mia? Hello? Can you still hear me?"

"Yeah, I hear you. Heard you. You want out of CP. Even though . . ."

"Even though what?" Helicity prompted when Mia didn't finish.

"Even though I'm in CP." Mia's voice suddenly had an edge to it. "And so are all our friends. If you move up, you won't be with us. Not in math, or science, or any other class."

Helicity sank deeper into the chair. "We don't know that for sure."

"Yeah, we do," Mia retorted.

"So how about you bump up, too?" Helicity regretted the suggestion the minute it came out of her mouth. Mia had dyslexia. She was clever and quick-witted, but because of her reading disability she had to work very hard just to keep up with her current course load.

Suggesting her friend move up to a more challenging level had been insensitive. Helicity fumbled to apologize, but Mia cut her off.

"Listen, I have to go. My—my grandmother is yelling at me to walk her dog again."

"Mia, wait!"

Helicity held her breath. Mia was her best friend. It was bad enough she'd inadvertently insulted her. She didn't want her to think she was going to abandon her. Not now, when their world was in such chaos. Not ever, actually.

After a long pause, Mia muttered, "What?"

"There's something neither of us thought of."

"Which is?"

Helicity plucked at a stray hair escaping from her braid. "I might bomb out on the exams even with the extra help. If I do"—she gave the hair a fierce yank, wincing at the sharp pain as it pulled free—"then it's game over."

CHAPTER ELEVEN

"This is unbelievable," Andy murmured. "I mean, you told me it was gone. But I didn't know it was . . . gone."

Helicity could only nod her agreement with her brother's statement. Her throat was too tight for words to pass through just then.

It was Saturday afternoon. Andy had been discharged from the hospital an hour earlier. At his insistence, he, Helicity, and their parents had driven in their new sedan, purchased the day before, to the spot where their house had once stood. After seeing the endless television coverage, newspaper photos, and some of the devastation up close, Helicity thought she'd be prepared to see what was left of their house.

But there was nothing left to see, except the hollow crater of their basement. Even the chimney was just a pile of bricks.

The kitchen where she'd made a surprise birthday cake for her father—gone. The living room where, years earlier, she and Andy made forts from couch cushions, chairs, and blankets—gone. The dining room where she'd joined hands with family and friends in thanks while smelling the mouthwatering turkey that awaited them—gone. And her sky-blue bedroom, with its glow-in-the-dark-star-studded ceiling, library of weather books, secret hiding place in the closet, and her big, comfortable bed just right for dreaming, day or night . . . gone.

They could and would rebuild, her father had told them. The new house would be bigger and better, everything brand-new and top-of-the-line. A house built just the way they wanted.

But what Helicity wanted were the familiar spaces packed to overflowing with memories. She didn't want a house. She wanted a home.

Drizzle filmed the windshield of their car and shrouded the place where their home had once been in gray mist. *It looks like I feel*, she thought. *Sad and empty inside.*

"Cleanup crews have been working nonstop," Mr. Dunlap informed them. "That's the only reason we were able to make it here. Before . . ." He shook his head and cracked a window.

Helicity recalled the images of her town buried beneath an avalanche of rubble and debris, the most hazardous areas cordoned off to keep people from digging through the ruins and endangering themselves. Despite the warnings, some people, desperate to salvage something of their former lives, had ventured in. Andy told her about one woman he'd seen at the hospital who'd slipped, fallen onto a broken window, and needed sixteen stitches to close the gaping wound in her abdomen.

Now, enough rubble had been cleared to make some areas reasonably safe. Their road was one such section. As they got out of the car, Helicity saw people walking through the shells of houses and buildings, poking into and sifting through the wreckage. They picked up stray items—a doll, a torn quilt, a baseball bat—and either tossed them aside or tucked them into tote bags, cardboard boxes, and plastic bins.

At least they're finding something, Helicity thought, staring at the basement hole again. There's nothing left for us to find.

Her father crossed his arms with determination. "We'll rebuild," he said again. "By the end of the summer, we'll be back here. Right now, though, it's time to show Andy our new place."

Earlier that morning, Helicity and her parents had moved into their rental house. It was a small three-bedroom ranch with one bathroom, a sitting room, a screened-in porch, and a tiny galley-style kitchen. The twin-size bed in Helicity's room was lumpy and the pillow smelled funny, but at least she had a room to herself. She and her mother spent a few hours cleaning the place from top to bottom before going to the hospital.

Helicity had visited Andy twice since school resumed. He still looked pretty banged up to her, but his doctor reported his injuries were healing well overall. Still, they sent him home with some prescription painkillers—and a strict warning to take them only if absolutely necessary.

Andy claimed he didn't need them. Yet he reached for the bottle soon after he was settled in his new bedroom.

"Hey, H," he called. "Bring your poor old brother some water, will you?"

"Your legs aren't broken, you know," she grumbled good-naturedly. But she got him a drink.

He swallowed a pill with a swig of water, then lay back. He sniffed and made a face. "My pillow smells funny."

Helicity grinned. "Yeah, mine too. Mom says she'll get us new ones tomorrow."

"Sit down," he commanded. "Fill me in on your life."

Helicity plunked into a hideous, floral-patterned easy chair that had seen better days. Before she started talking, she glanced at the open door. Andy raised his eyebrows.

"Got something to hide from Mom and Dad?" he stage-whispered.

Helicity hesitated, then nudged the door with her

foot so it swung closed. "It's not that I'm hiding any-thing," she said. "I just haven't told them something I'm doing."

"Is this something you're doing naughty and dan-gerous?"

She rolled her eyes. "Of course not! It's just, some people have been helping me so I can do well on my finals next week." She told him about Lana and Sam.

Andy looked puzzled. "Why wouldn't you tell Mom and Dad about that?" He held up his good hand. "Wait. I already know the answer. If you tell them and you don't do well, you'll feel like a failure."

"I hadn't thought of it that way, actually, but now that you mention it—yeah. The truth is, if I do ace the exams, I'm going to ask them to let me take honors next year."

Andy grinned. "No kidding!" He shrugged, then winced and gingerly rubbed his shoulder. "Stupid painkillers take forever to work. Makes me want to take another." He dropped his hand. "Listen, H, I say go for it. Who knows? Maybe this Laura woman will become your mentor or something."

"Lana," Helicity corrected. "And what's a mentor?"

"Someone who takes you under her wing, guides you along your path to greatness, that sort of thing." Andy gave a big yawn. "Anyway, your secret is safe with me. Though if I ever hear of that Sam kid trying anything with you—"

"Andy!" Helicity blushed to the roots of her hair.

"Just saying he'll have to answer to your big brother. Busted arm or no busted arm, he wouldn't like that. Now shoo. I have some sleeping to do."

"Time's up."

Helicity scribbled one last answer on her test, then put her pencil down, laid her head on the desk, and groaned.

"That doesn't sound positive." Sam whisked the papers away. "But let's see how you did." He flopped onto Lana's spare office chair and started going over her work.

It was late Wednesday afternoon, and Helicity was exhausted. Sam had pushed her hard the last two days to grasp the physical science concepts of force, waves, matter, and energy. When Lana overheard her struggling, she stepped in and broke the concepts into smaller, more manageable parts. Sam drilled her on math, too, until Helicity felt like her head would explode if she stuffed one more equation in it.

Her studies weren't the only thing tiring her out. That morning, instead of going to regular classes, she went to a counseling session with a handful of other middle school students. Like her, they had lost their homes or the bulk of their possessions in the tornado. Because she'd known them for years, Helicity could tell the losses and the tragedy had affected them. Many seemed to be just staying afloat in a churning sea of emotions—anger, fear, panic. Others tried their best to pretend they were fine. But Helicity wasn't fooled. She knew what was going on in their heads because she had felt the same things—was still feeling them—herself.

The young counselor did his best to get them to talk about their emotions. No one really opened up, though, which didn't surprise Helicity. Kids her age tended to communicate with sarcasm and ridicule, not open honesty, and sharing emotions while their peers were watching and listening was far down their list of things to do. Most spent the hour slouched in their chairs, shuffling their feet, grunting monosyllabic replies to the man's probing questions, and glancing repeatedly at the clock. Helicity herself used the time to mentally prepare for the tests Sam planned to give her that afternoon.

Now those tests were done. She felt drained, as if all the knowledge she'd been storing up for the past week had poured out of her through her pencil. Only time—and Sam—would tell whether she'd used that knowledge correctly.

While she waited for Sam to grade her test, she thumbed through her texts. There was one from Andy, asking how she'd done and telling her he'd back her up with her folks if they gave her any grief. He also reminded her that he'd pulverize Sam if Sam so much as looked at her funny. There were other texts from her friend group chat, which she scanned but didn't join in on. Another was from Lana, asking them to lock up when they were done since she would be in a meeting for the rest of the day—and to contact her once Sam had graded the tests.

Helicity was sending a reply acknowledging that

she'd do as Lana requested when her phone pinged with an urgent message from Mia.

CALL ME!!!

Helicity sucked in her breath. Mia had texted her in all caps just once before, when she found out her parents were divorcing. That she used all caps now could only mean one thing: something major had happened. Good or bad, she didn't know.

But before she could text Mia, Sam's phone suddenly blared. He jumped up, scattering Helicity's test papers, and yanked it out of his pocket. He stared at the screen, then cried, "Yes!" and rushed to the office door.

"Wait!" Helicity cried, also jumping to her feet. "Where are you going? What about my exams?"

"I've got something more important to do!"

"What? What's more important than grading my papers?"

"Chasing a storm." Sam paused with his hand on the doorknob and looked back at her with a broad grin. "Want to watch?"

CHAPTER TWELVE

Helicity's stomach did an excited flip-flop. "You mean I can go with you?"

"What? God, no. Lana would kill me if I took a newbie on a ride-along." Sam grabbed the computer keyboard and typed in a command. A map of Michigan appeared on the screen. Scattered across it were tiny black car icons. He moused over to one and zoomed in. "That's my car. When it turns white, click on it. Bye!"

"Wait! Where—"

But Sam was gone.

Helicity gathered her test papers but kept one eye

on the screen. Then she remembered Mia's text. Just as she thumbed to reply, Sam's car icon turned white. She put down her phone and clicked the icon. A small window popped up next to the car. *Live stream?* it asked.

"Yes, I guess," she muttered, clicking the appropriate button.

A video feed, unfocused at first, resolved itself to show the college's entrance gate looming up ahead. As the gate drew closer, Helicity realized she was seeing it from the dashboard of Sam's car, a beat-up old baby-blue sedan he drove to and from the school.

"Hey, Fourteen!"

Helicity started as Sam's voice, a tinny echo as if coming from inside a soup can, suddenly streamed through the computer's speakers.

"I don't know if you're watching, but here's the deal. I got a severe thunderstorm warning—there's some nasty stuff brewing over Lake Michigan just west of here. I'm thinking serious straight-line wind action. So that's where I'm headed. Sorry I couldn't take you along with me, but like I said, Lana would have killed me if I had. Maybe next time, though! Okay, I'm signing off until I get a little closer to the storm."

The video cut off, replaced by a message informing her the livestreaming was no longer active.

Nasty stuff? Helicity snatched up her phone and opened her radar app. She zoomed in on the section of Lake Michigan's shoreline directly west of the college. Sure enough, a long, bow-shaped line of storms was stretching across almost half the lake due west of them.

She hit Animate. Now she could see the storm lurching toward the shore—no, not lurching, but racing. The southern and northern edge even appeared to take on a curl, almost like the end of a hipster's mustache.

The red, green, and yellow radar image froze, reset, and replayed the storm's progress over that time span again. She hit another button that allowed her to track the storm's timing. It was less than an hour from her and a half hour from the shore.

She glanced back at Lana's computer. Sam's car icon was on a major highway, heading directly toward the storm. More specifically, the *red* area of the storm. Meaning the heaviest rain and the most danger.

That's just what he wants, she thought. To be

in the thick of it. I wish I could be there with him.

Suddenly, she sat up.

I should be with him. Or if not me, then someone else.

Weather junkie that she was, Helicity followed several blogs and devoured any articles written by experienced storm chasers. Nearly all advised the same thing: never chase alone. You couldn't watch the road, other drivers, and the weather at the same time; for that, you needed at least two pairs of eyes.

It was possible that Sam planned to pick up someone to go with him. But somehow, Helicity didn't think so.

Sam's car icon turned white again. "I'm just about to hit the nose of the storm," he announced when she resumed streaming. "According to the GPS, there's a dirt road ahead that leads to a little beach."

A thick black line swept across the screen. There was a thump, and the line swept back again, leaving behind a clearer image.

The windshield wipers, Helicity realized. Sam was cleaning the windshield before the big reveal. She ignored the wipers and focused on what was happening beyond the glass.

The video veered and jumped as Sam turned off the highway, onto the dirt road. Low-hanging tree branches slapped against the windshield. The image skipped violently downward, then jolted back up, as if the car had nosedived into and climbed out of a shallow ditch.

"Whoops! Almost broke an axle in that rut!" Sam said with a laugh.

Then the picture stilled, and Helicity had a wide-open view of Lake Michigan through the windshield.

"Whoa." She and Sam uttered the word at the same moment.

Gunmetal-gray clouds hung over the water. The shelf cloud was huge. It stretched west to east as far as the eye could see; the top was bright white and the base almost black. That white top curled over in a menacing, almost toothlike way. It was a true monster. The wind had already started whipping up white-crested waves that hammered the thin sliver of beachfront. A seagull flew into view, made the scene appear so serene for a moment, and then soared backward and away.

"Look at that," Sam said.

"I'm looking," Helicity replied, forgetting that Sam couldn't hear her.

"Looking at what?" a voice behind her asked.

Helicity yelped and spun around to find Lana coming in the office. "Lana! What are you doing here? I thought you were in a meeting."

"It ended sooner than— Wait a minute." Lana stared at the computer screen and frowned. "Sam?"

"Yeah," Helicity answered. "He saw the storm over Lake Michigan and . . . and . . ." She faltered because Lana's brow suddenly furrowed more deeply.

"Tell me he's not alone. Never mind, I already know the answer." Lana slapped her palm on the desktop, making a stray pencil jump and roll off. "Damn it, Sam! I told you never to—"

Slam!

Lana tensed at the sound from the computer speakers. "And now he's gotten out of the car. Jesus."

Sure enough, Sam appeared on the screen. He had an expensive-looking digital camera around his neck. He grinned at the dash cam and then spun to face the lake. Then he kicked off his boots and ran into the water with the camera bouncing on his chest. He flung his arms open wide, as if inviting the storm to come get him, then lifted the camera to his eye and started clicking away.

Lana swore and snatched up Helicity's phone. "May I? Mine's buried in my bag." She dialed Sam's number without waiting for Helicity to reply. A second later, they heard his ring tone through the speakers. Lana cursed again. "Really? He left it in the car? What teenager doesn't keep his phone with him?"

The phone stopped ringing. Lana barked, "Call me, you idiot," when Sam's voice mail kicked on. She hung up and wheeled around to Helicity.

"There are rules when storm chasing," she growled. "Like, don't leave your vehicle and stay in communication. Oh, and how about avoid dirt roads?"

Helicity nodded. "And don't go alone."

Lana pointed a finger at her. "Exactly! Thank you!"

Helicity stared at the floor. "I wanted to go with him."

Lana went on as if Helicity hadn't spoken. "Oh, and here's the most important one." She glared at Sam, who had stopped photographing the storm and was now flailing his arms and whooping loud enough for the dash camera's microphone to pick up. *"Use your common sense!"*

They watched in silence as Sam danced along the shoreline and kicked sand into the waves, as playful as a little boy and seemingly oblivious to the imminent rain and wind that would soak him and his camera.

"Hey. The storm's going to pass quickly—and maybe not be quite as bad," Helicity suddenly said.

Lana gave her a curious look. "What makes you say that?"

Helicity indicated a section of the screen. "See right here? The clouds aren't as dark or as low. It looks like it's almost lifting."

As Helicity talked, Lana nodded slowly, her gaze darting around the screen as she followed Helicity's observations.

A few moments later, Sam seemed to notice the changes, too. He stopped frolicking. Hands on hips facing the storm, he kicked the sand again. But this time, the movement looked frustrated. He sloshed out of the water, grabbed his boots, and returned to the car. A gust of wind and a moderate rain followed.

"So much for that." His voice was thick with

disappointment. A close-up of his hand appeared, and the video jerked around to show him sitting sideways in the driver's seat, sandy feet outside the open car door. He pulled a towel from the backseat and rubbed it over his wet hair, making it stick up even more than usual, then wiped off the digital camera. "Helicity, if you—or anybody else—is watching, here's a little FYI for you: this happens a lot in storm chasing. Especially over the lake. There's a big storm, looks like something major could develop, then *pffft*! You get a shower."

He used the towel to brush the sand from his feet. "Oh, well. At least I didn't tell Lana about it. Speaking of which . . . Fourteen, do me a favor and keep my adventure our little secret, okay? Lana hates when I— That is, she hates false alarms."

Lana gave a derisive laugh-snort. "Yeah, *that's* what I hate."

Sam retrieved his phone from the passenger seat. "Oh, sorry, looks like I missed your call." He dialed into his voice mail.

"This should be interesting," Lana muttered.

Sam's eyes suddenly widened. "Oh, crap." He made

a face and reached for the dash cam. The last thing Helicity saw on the live stream was his hand. Then the screen flickered to the map with the car icons. *Live stream ended*, the caption informed her as Sam's car, now black, slowly retraced its path back to the highway.

Lana shook her head and sighed. She picked up the pencil from the floor, pulled Helicity's exams closer, and began correcting them. For a few minutes, the only sound was the rustle of paper and the scratch of the pencil. Then Lana spoke.

"You seem to know a bit about storm chasing."

Helicity gave a modest shrug. "I've been reading up on it, is all."

"Mmm." Lana continued correcting the exam. "You know, I was your age when I went on my first chase."

"My age? Seriously?"

"Yup."

"What was it like?"

Lana smiled. "About what Sam just experienced. Full of excited anticipation as we made our forecast. Then a big letdown when the storm petered out. But that didn't stop me from trying again. And again. I spent the whole summer learning the ropes from a team of chasers."

She pointed the pencil at the photo of the mothership cloud formation hovering over the farmhouse. "I took that with a cheap little point-and-shoot camera. That's all I had back then. There were sixteen shots left on the roll of film, and I used them all up in about twenty seconds trying to get one really good shot. That's the best one. When my team leader saw the print, he gave me this." With a faraway smile etched in memory, she touched the lightning bolt necklace she always wore.

She went back to correcting Helicity's exams, but kept talking. "So . . . you wanted to go with Sam, huh?"

Helicity blinked. She didn't think Lana had heard her say that. "Yes."

"Why?"

The question took Helicity off guard. "I thought it would be exciting, I guess."

Lana stilled. "I see."

Helicity pulled at the end of her braid. "But it was more than that."

Lana turned to face her. "Go on."

Helicity shifted in her seat, trying to find the words to explain. "I've been caught in a lot of storms. I guess I wanted to go after one for once. To do the catching instead of being caught. I want to learn. And then there's this feeling I get when I'm in wild weather. Like . . . like I'm in my element, doing what I'm meant to do. Joy, my brother calls it." She gave a self-conscious laugh. "Bet that sounds stupid, huh?"

"Not in the least." Lana's voice was serious. "I feel that, too. But I'm surprised, I guess. I would have thought your experience with the tornado . . ." She left the sentence unfinished.

Helicity looked at the floor. "I don't ever want to go through that again," she admitted. "But seeing one from a safe distance, watching as it develops, understanding why it behaves the way it does, knowing that what I learn from it could help save lives someday . . . I don't think I'll ever stop wanting to do that."

Lana's gaze drifted to the newspaper clipping on her bulletin board, the one with the headline STORM CHASER CHEATS DEATH. "I won't either. But I definitely respect it more than ever. One missed cue—one navigational error—and the chasers can become the chased. And suddenly, what started out being exciting turns dangerous. Even the most experienced scientists and researchers can run into trouble. And if you're reckless . . ." She shook her head, and Helicity knew she was thinking of Sam.

The computer screen suddenly shifted to slideshow mode. Helicity's photos of the tornado flashed by. Her mind flooded with images of the devastation it had left in its wake.

"I know storm chasing can be dangerous," she murmured. "And that it can be boring and frustrating, too. But I still want to do it someday."

Lana suddenly spun in her chair to face Helicity full-on. She leaned forward and stared at her intently, as if trying to reach deep into her mind. Then just as suddenly, she smiled.

"Well, then, Helicity Dunlap, granddaughter of Doris Picossi," she said. "What would you say if I told you that 'someday' might be sooner than you think?"

CHAPTER THIRTEEN

"Me? On your team? *Seriously?*"

Lana laughed. Helicity noted what a gorgeous laugh she had. "For the second time, yes! I'm leading a storm-chasing team to the northern plains this summer, and I'd like you to be part of that team."

Emotion threatened to overwhelm Helicity. "But I'm only thirteen!"

"Fourteen this summer though, right?" Lana said with a twinkle in her eye. She touched her lightning bolt necklace. "Like I said, same age I was when I started. The trip won't be glamourous—cheap hotels, fast food—and we may not even encounter any significant weather events. And you may not be on the front line of any events that do blow up. But I guarantee you'll learn the right way to chase storms, and you'll discover whether it's something you're cut out for—or even like."

"Oh, I'll like it," Helicity told her enthusiastically. "I just can't believe you're really inviting me!"

Lana pulled a folder from a file on her desk and handed it to Helicity. "This is information about our summer plans. Take it home. Read it. Share it with your parents. Have them call me with any questions or concerns. And of course, you do the same. In the meantime"—she added Helicity's corrected exams to the folder—"congratulations. You got a ninety-six on the science part and a ninety-three on the math. But you still have your real tests tomorrow, so study hard tonight and get a good night's sleep."

Helicity hugged the folder to her chest. She doubted she would get any sleep that night, not with a summer of storm chasing dangling in front of her.

* * *

Floating on air, Helicity crossed to the campus parking lot, where her mother was waiting for her in the car.

"You look like you had a good day," her mother observed on the ride home.

"Yeah. I did." Helicity wanted to tell her mother about Lana's invitation, but on the walk to the car she'd decided to hold off until she'd talked with Andy. He always knew the right way to manipulate their parents into doing what he wanted, and she wanted some tips. Learn a little of that Andy charm.

They pulled into the driveway of their rental home a few minutes later. A bike was leaning against the side of the garage. Mia sat on the ground next to it, throwing pebbles into a rusty can. Helicity's good mood vanished in a swirl of guilt.

"Shoot, shoot, shoot, shoot!" She leaped out of the car and hurried over. "Mia! I'm so sorry! I forgot—"

Mia jumped up, laughing. "Yeah, I figured as much. That's why I came to you. Listen, I've got news. Oh, hey, Mrs. D!"

"Hello, Mia," Mrs. Dunlap returned. "Stay for dinner?"

"Thanks, but no. Mom and Gram are expecting me back."

"Okay, see you soon." Helicity's mother disappeared inside.

"Mmm, maybe not," Mia said with a gleam in her eye.

Helicity hadn't seen her friend so excited for months. "All right, what is going on?"

"I'm going to Texas!"

Helicity's jaw dropped. "What? Why? When? With who?"

Mia laughed. "Yikes, reel it in, girlfriend, and give me a chance to talk!" They sat down together and Mia explained.

"So now that my folks are officially divorced, my mom is going through this whole self-discovery phase." She rolled her eyes. "Whatever. My therapist told me it might happen and that I should be supportive of Mom's 'journey.'" She put the word *journey* in air quotes. "Anyway, Mom decided the best way I could support her is to go stay with my aunt—her sister—in Texas for the summer."

"She's sending you away? That's a little harsh," Helicity observed.

"Yeah, except my aunt has this *gorgeous* house right on the Gulf of Mexico. It's a bed-and-breakfast, actually, and I'll be helping her run it this summer. You know, cleaning rooms, making and serving breakfast, that sort of thing." Mia rubbed her fingers together. "She's paying me *and* I get to keep any tips the guests leave."

Helicity grinned. "You? Clean rooms? *Cook?*"

Mia grinned back. "Yeah, I know, right? Anyway, Mom and I are flying down next week, then Mom's flying back—and I'm staying until the end of August!" Her grin faded. "You're not mad, are you? That I'm leaving for the summer?"

"No, because guess what? I'm leaving, too! If my parents agree, anyway." She quickly filled Mia in on Lana's offer.

Mia was so excited for her she started flapping her hands in the air. "You *have* to go on that trip," she cried. "Seriously! Maybe that hottie Sam is going, too." She raised her eyebrows and smirked, then stood up, grabbed Helicity's backpack, and held it out. "What are you waiting for? Go! Talk to Andy right now! Then do whatever you have to do to convince your folks! Speaking of which . . ." She checked her phone and made a face. "I gotta pedal or I'll be late for dinner." She wheeled her bike away from the garage and hopped on. "Call me later!"

"I will!"

Helicity watched Mia ride away. Then, holding her backpack tightly, she headed inside to find Andy.

Loud voices coming from the living room stopped her in her tracks.

"I'm telling you, he is in pain!" her father said. "He needs more of those meds!"

"Joe," Mrs. Dunlap replied tightly, "the doctor warned—"

"The *doctor*." Her father spat the word. "Is she seeing what our boy is going through? Has she even called to check up on him since he left the hospital? No! Look at him, Elizabeth!"

Helicity crept down the front hall past the kitchen and peeked into the living room.

Andy was stretched out on the couch. His head sagged back as if it cost him too much effort to hold it up. The weak afternoon light filtering through the dusty curtains revealed gray smudgy hollows under his eyes. Mr. Dunlap stood next to him, glaring at his wife. She crossed her arms and bowed her head as if she was closing herself off from his anger.

"He's pushing himself too hard through those rehab exercises," Mr. Dunlap said. "He needs relief afterward."

"Dad, it's okay," Andy intervened. "I'll just take some over-the-counter stuff." Yet when he moved to get up, his face contorted with pain, and he fell back onto the pillows.

"That's it." Helicity's father grabbed his phone. "I'm getting him help. If his own doctor won't prescribe what he needs, I'll find one who will." He stalked into the master bedroom and slammed the door.

Mrs. Dunlap sank down next to the couch and stroked Andy's hair. "How bad is it, honey?"

"On a scale of one to ten?" Andy closed his eyes and turned his head away. "It's an eleven, Mom."

She looked at him for a long moment and seemed about to say something. But whatever it was, was cut off when Mr. Dunlap emerged from the bedroom, practically shouting into the phone.

"Joe!" Mrs. Dunlap admonished. "Don't—"

"Back off, Elizabeth," her father warned.

Helicity quickly backpedaled to the front door, stepped outside, and closed it behind her with a quiet click. She sank down on the stoop and, with a sigh, pulled out the folder Lana had given her.

Not exactly the best time to share my news, she thought.

"Hey, Fourteen!"

Helicity started at the sound of Sam's voice. She had been so engrossed in her thoughts she hadn't heard him drive up. Now his car idled at the side of the road, and he leaned out of the driver's side window. With his sunglasses, leather jacket, old-model sedan, and killer smile, he looked like a 1950s movie star.

She jumped to her feet and hurried over. "What are you doing here?"

"I swung by to congratulate you, for one thing."

Helicity blinked in confusion. "For what?"

"I just came from the college. Lana ordered me back to face the music. Dum, dum, dummmmmm." He pretended to play heavy chords of dramatic music on the dashboard.

"Was that okay?" Helicity asked cautiously. "She seemed pretty mad."

Sam waved away her concern. "Meh, Lana's anger is like lightning. Quick flash and then it's gone."

Helicity chose not to point out how dangerous lightning could be. If Lana's anger was anything like that . . .

"Anyway," Sam continued, "after she finished chewing me out, she told me that you might be joining our team this summer. Can't say I'm surprised. I knew she liked you right from the start. In fact, I was a little worried that she liked you better than me. But then I realized that was impossible because I am the best." He took off his sunglasses and winked up at her, causing her breath to catch in her throat for a second. "So what did your family say when you told them?"

"Uh, I haven't yet." She glanced over her shoulder at the front door. "Things are a little . . . complicated . . . right now."

"Want me to talk to them?" he offered.

"No, that's okay, I—"

"Seriously, I'll talk to them." Sam started to get out. "It's not a problem."

"No!" She hadn't meant to shout. But she didn't want Sam to walk in on her family arguing. Plus she wasn't sure what they'd make of him. Compared to Andy, Sam looked like a rebel—a bad boy they might not want her to hang out with.

"I mean, no thanks," she said. "I'll take care of it." Then something he'd said registered. "Wait . . . *our* team?"

CHAPTER FOURTEEN

"**D**idn't Lana tell you, Fourteen? She invited me to come along this summer, too."

With that news, Helicity's anxiety about her parents and her brother took a backseat to a sudden flutter of happiness. She knew she was grinning like an idiot, but she couldn't help it. "That's so awesome!"

Sam laughed. "No kidding, huh? I'm pretty stoked about it. So hurry up and get your parents' signatures, will you?"

"You know it. In fact, I'll go right now and—"

"Whoops, hang on. I almost forgot something."

Sam fished a crumpled envelope out of his pocket and held it out to her. "Here's the other reason I stopped by."

Mystified, Helicity took the envelope and looked inside. Her eyes widened. "Money? I don't understand. Why are you giving me your money?"

"Not *my* money, Fourteen. Yours."

"Huh?"

Sam grinned broadly. "Congratulations. You sold two of your tornado photos."

"Sold my photos?" Helicity shook her head, now totally confused. "No, I didn't."

Sam laughed. "Okay, technically, *I* sold your photos. Prints of them, that is. Now don't be mad," he added hastily. "There's this old guy in the nursing home where my dad works who collects tornado photos. He's kind of a nut, but harmless. I hang out with him sometimes and we talk weather stuff. Anyway, I showed him your pics two days ago, and he almost fell out of his wheelchair, he was so eager to have them. Paid a decent amount right then and there."

Sam withdrew the money from the envelope and

fanned it out to show her three twenties, a ten, and a five. "Not bad, huh?"

Helicity stared at the bills, her mind still trying to wrap around what Sam was telling her. "You sold copies of my photos for seventy-five dollars?"

Sam cleared his throat uncomfortably. "Well, he paid a hundred for the pair, actually. I, um, kept twenty-five as a finder's fee. Business is business, after all."

"I don't care about that." Helicity eyed the money with growing discomfort. "I just— Sam, I feel a little weird about your selling my photos, I guess. I mean . . . shouldn't you have asked me first?"

Sam put his sunglasses back on. "Okay, first of all, I thought I was doing you a favor. I would have killed to have seventy-five bucks handed to me when I was your age. Secondly, it all happened so fast, there wasn't time to contact you. And third, lots of storm chasers make money by selling photos." He looked her up and down and shrugged. "But I guess you're too young and inexperienced to understand that."

His words stung. She bit her lip and shook her head. "I—I know I have a lot to learn. So I guess . . . thank you for this." She held up the money.

He waved her thanks away and started the car. But before he took off, he held out his hand and gave her a wide smile. "Still friends?"

She tucked the money in her pocket and took his hand. "Yeah." Though she still felt a little uneasy about what he'd done, she didn't want there to be friction between them—especially if they ended up spending time together that summer. "Still friends."

He thumped the side of his car. "Good luck on your exams tomorrow, Fourteen!" Then he revved the engine and took off, leaving her standing in a cloud of dust.

Helicity barely tasted her pasta that night. Her mind whirled with a jumble of emotions—elation over Lana's invitation, happiness for Mia, concern for Andy, and confusion over what Sam had done. Her mood wasn't helped by her parents' curt conversation, which made the air thick with tension.

Only Andy was lively and talkative. In fact, he seemed like a completely different person than the one she'd seen on the couch earlier. She shot him an inquisitive look, and he mimed swallowing a pill. Then she understood. He was happy because he wasn't in pain—not at the moment, anyway. Fortunately, his good mood thawed the iciness in the air, and by dessert time, her mother and father were behaving as if their argument had never happened.

Still, Helicity chose to stick to her plan of talking to Andy about Lana's offer before approaching her parents. So after she'd cleared the table and put the dishes in the dishwasher, she cornered her brother in his bedroom.

"Hey, Hel!" he cried as if he'd never been happier to see someone in his life.

She laughed, shaking her head. "Sheesh, how many of those pain meds did you take? Listen, I need to talk to you about something."

He pulled his legs in to make room for her at the end of the bed. "I'm all ears. At least until I fall asleep. Then I'm all snores."

"Shut up and listen, will you?" Helicity growled. She brought him up to date on Lana's invitation, her solid grades on the practice tests, and on Mia's summer plans. She told him what she knew about the storm-chasing excursion, handing him the folder as she did so.

"Well, one thing Dad will like," he observed as he scanned the contents. "The trip is funded by some group called the LME Foundation. So you won't have to pay for anything except stuff you want to buy for yourself." He smiled. "You might have to smash open your piggy bank."

"Or not." Helicity withdrew the money Sam had given her.

Andy whistled. "Whoa, where'd you get that much cash?"

Helicity told him what had happened. Andy narrowed his eyes. "And this guy is going on the trip, too? He sounds . . . iffy."

"No, he's okay," Helicity reassured him. She stuffed the money back into her pocket.

"Well, if you say so." Andy tossed the papers aside. "But Hel, you *sure* you want to spend the whole summer driving around with people you barely know?"

"I've never wanted to do anything so much in my life," she replied earnestly. "Sam is energetic and smart. He'll be fun to hang out with. And Lana is the best. You'd really like her."

"It doesn't matter if *I* like Lana," Andy pointed out. "Or Sam."

"I know. Mom and Dad have to." Helicity let out a deep sigh. "So how do I get my dream summer to happen?"

"You gotta build up to it." Andy tapped her practice exams. "First, ace your finals. Then let Mom and Dad know that your high scores wouldn't have been possible without Lana and Sam. After that, start dropping hints about how bored you're going to be this summer with Mia gone. I'll chime in that I'll be too busy with rehab and stuff to drive you anywhere, which means you'll be stuck on your own in this dump day after day. Work in how you don't expect them to entertain you because you know how busy they're going to be."

He shot her a crafty smile. "Once those seeds have been planted, you go in for the kill—invite Lana to dinner to meet Mom and Dad. If she's as great as you say she is, they'll approve of her, and you'll be good to go."

Helicity looked at him admiringly. "How do

you come up with such an awesome plan so quickly?"

He gave an imperious sniff. "Hello? I'm a quarter-back, remember? I'm trained to see all the options and make the best one happen."

"Okay, but what if the plan *doesn't* succeed?" Helicity prodded.

Andy lay back on his pillows. "Simple. You punt—and hope for the best."

CHAPTER FIFTEEN

Helicity didn't have to put Andy's plan in motion, or punt, either. After her last exam on Friday, she headed to her mother's office as usual. She'd just pushed open the glass door when, to her great surprise, she heard Lana's voice coming from the back room. She froze and listened.

"—a bright young girl who has demonstrated to me a keen interest in and surprising knowledge of meteorology and storm-chasing concepts," Lana said. "She'd truly be an asset to my team and would learn a great deal, too."

"Yes, but she's so young," Mrs. Dunlap protested. "And what she's been through—"

"—has not quelled her fascination with weather one bit," Lana finished. "If anything, Mrs. Dunlap—"

"Elizabeth."

"Elizabeth. If anything, her experience has added weight to her passion. The tornado is a tragedy no one in your town or this state will ever forget. But only a few will actively look to *learn* from it. I'm one of those few. Helicity is another. She's processing what happened. She wants to understand. Not just for the sake of knowledge, but so in the future she can help." Lana paused, and then added in a surprisingly wistful tone, "I don't have children. But if I ever do, I hope they'll be like her."

Sudden tears pricked Helicity's eyes and a lump formed in her throat. She swallowed hard a few times, then pitched her voice to sound cheerful. "Mom? Mom, you here?"

Her mother and Lana emerged from the back office. Helicity put on her best surprised face. "Lana? Mom? What's going on?"

"Dr. McElvoy—" her mother started to say.

"Lana, please," Lana interrupted with a smile.

"Lana came by to convince me to let you join her this summer," Helicity's mother said. "I must admit, I was a bit disappointed the information came from her and not you."

"I know, I know, I should have told you," Helicity admitted. "But there never seemed to be the right time. Now that you know, though . . . did she convince you?"

Her mother folded her arms over her chest and gave her a stern look, but Helicity saw a smile tug at her lips. "She made a good case. But before I sign any forms, we need to discuss everything with your father."

When she got home, Helicity went to work arranging things designed to put her father in a good mood. She made his favorite summertime dessert—strawberry shortcake—and mixed up lemonade to have with their burgers, tossed salad, and chips. Because he enjoyed the breeze on the screened-in porch, she set the picnic table so they could eat there. When she heard his truck, she opened a bottle of beer to hand him when he walked in.

"Pouring it on a little thick, aren't you?" Andy muttered from his usual spot on the couch.

"Shush! He'll hear— Hey, Daddy! Welcome home!" Helicity gave him the beer and followed it up with a tight hug.

Mr. Dunlap squeezed her back, took a long sip of beer, sniffed the shortcake-scented air, and said, "Right. What do you want?"

Andy burst out laughing. "Told you!"

"Told him what?" Helicity's mother said, coming in from the grill with a plate of juicy burgers.

"Helicity wants something from me," her husband informed her. "So what is it, kiddo? Money? A puppy? New sneakers?"

His tone was so jovial that Helicity just blurted it out. "I've been invited to go on a storm-chasing trip this summer. Can I go? Please?"

And just like that, her father's good mood evaporated. "Storm chasing?" Mouth tight, he put the beer bottle down with a *thunk*. "I gotta hit the can. Start eating without me." He disappeared into the bathroom, leaving Helicity standing rigid with disappointment.

Mrs. Dunlap set the burgers on the table and hurried to Helicity's side. "Oh, baby, I—"

"I'm *not* a baby," Helicity said through gritted teeth. Steely resolve surged through her with the sudden force of a flash flood, forcing out the disappointment. "I'm a survivor, and *I am going on that trip*."

She broke away from her mother and strode to the bathroom.

"Hel," Andy warned, "I wouldn't do that if I—"

Helicity knocked on the door.

"Occupied!" her father growled from within.

"Dad, it's me." Helicity's voice was tight with determination. "I know you think my interest in the weather is a joke. But it's important to me. So important that I've been getting tutored every afternoon so I can grasp the science and math behind it. And I *am* grasping it. Two days ago, I took practice tests and aced them. I finished my school finals today, and I'm pretty sure I aced them, too. Even if I didn't, I want to move up from CP to honors-level classes next year."

Her mother made a noise in her throat, but Helicity ignored her.

"This *trip* is important to me, too, because I'll get to

explore my—my *passion* for weather with people who feel the same way about it. It's not going to cost you a cent, and I'll be learning and experiencing things no class at school can ever teach me. You, Mom, and Andy won't have time for me this summer, and Mia's going away, which leaves me sitting around doing nothing. So I'm asking you again—*can I go?*"

She stared at the closed door, waiting. There was silence, then the toilet flushed, water ran in the sink, and the door opened. She stared up at her father, knowing she was blocking his exit but refusing to move.

Slowly, he reached forward and cupped his calloused hand under her chin. His mouth worked, and he gazed at her with an expression she'd never seen on his face before, at least not when he was looking at her. Pride. It was pride.

"You know, I never realized it until just now, but there's a fighter in there, isn't there?" he said softly.

She nodded against his hand.

He looked over at Helicity's mother. "This woman . . . you trust her to watch out for our daughter?"

"As if Helicity were her own child," Mrs. Dunlap replied.

Helicity's father moved his hand to the top of her head and smoothed her hair. His eyes locked with hers. Then he pulled her to him and wrapped her in his arms.

"I'll miss you. Probably more than you know," he murmured. "But yes. You can go."

Helicity burrowed her face in his chest and whispered, "Thank you." They stood like that for a long moment. Then Andy broke the spell.

"Dang," he drawled. "Those burgers smell great, Mom. So how about we celebrate Helicity leaving by chowing down?"

CHAPTER SIXTEEN

The following two weeks whizzed by in a blur of paperwork, preparations, and good-byes. In addition to the forms Lana needed, Helicity's parents signed the high school override, allowing her to bump up to the honors classes. Two nights before Mia left for Texas, they had a sleepover—or as Mrs. Dunlap called it, "a no-sleep sleepover," because the girls talked so late into the night. They parted the next morning with tearful hugs and promises to text or call each other as often as possible.

At Lana's insistence, Helicity spent one afternoon the following week taking a crash course in storm spotting offered by NOAA, the National Oceanic and Atmospheric Administration.

"I suspect you know almost as much as the instructors," she told Helicity. "Still, there may be gaps in your understanding. This program goes step-by-step, so it should fill in those gaps. Plus, I'd feel better, knowing you'd gone through the course."

Helicity enjoyed the training more than she'd expected. It gave her confidence in her own knowledge and taught her a few things she didn't know, too.

"Guess how many inches of water it takes to pull an adult off his feet," she challenged Andy that night.

"Uh, gee, let's see . . . a billion?"

"Six," she corrected. "Just six inches if it's moving superfast, like in a flash flood. Twelve inches can sweep away a small car. Twenty-four inches if it's a big car."

"Wow. I just realized something." Andy stared at her in amazement. "You are a complete and total geek!"

"Oh, shut up," she grumbled.

Two days later, Helicity took Raven out for a ride, their first since the tornado. She gave the horse his head, and he made for the hillside trail as if he knew that's where she longed to go. Someone had cleared the fallen tree from the path, but the broken stump with its jagged tips remained. She shivered as they trotted past, remembering how close they'd come to being hit.

She dismounted when they reached the top. Raven wandered to his favorite patch of grass to graze, and she climbed the boulder and gazed down at the landscape far below.

Her town was mending, but it was still a far cry from full recovery. Construction vehicles—some of them from her father's company—moved about the streets and through wreckage and rubble. From where she stood, they looked like toys driven by some unseen child's hand. Lines of people snaked through the high school parking lot to the relief vehicles stocked with medical supplies and everyday necessities. A long gouge in the earth outside of town showed where the tornado had touched down and traveled on its destructive journey.

A few miles east or west, Helicity thought, and it might have missed us completely.

She didn't take photos. She didn't need to, for the

sights before her were seared into her memory. As she rode Raven back down the hill and to the farm, she vowed never to forget them—and to do all she could to help prevent such devastation from destroying other lives in the future.

The morning of her departure, Helicity got up at the crack of dawn. Lana and Sam were due to pick her up at eight thirty. Then they'd drive northwest to the coastal town of Muskegon, where they'd board the midmorning ferry and cross Lake Michigan to Milwaukee, Wisconsin. She'd packed the night before with her mother's help and using a list Lana had provided of what to bring and what to leave behind.

Now she cleaned out her purse so her wallet—filled with the seventy-five dollars Sam had given her—and her phone would fit easily inside. She zipped the purse closed and left it on the dresser. Then she opened her suitcase to add one last item: the notebook Mia had given her. She'd been too busy to write anything in it yet, but last night she'd decided to bring it to record everything that happened on her trip.

"Didn't you check your suitcase, like, five times last night?" a voice from behind her asked.

She turned to find Andy standing in her doorway, rubbing the sleep from his eyes. "If you don't have something helpful to say, why don't you go back to bed?" she replied with a grin.

"What, and miss the chance to see you leave? No way." He yawned widely. "Seriously, though, Hel . . . it's going to be pretty quiet around here without you. I might even—dare I say it?—miss you."

Helicity looked up from the shirt she was refolding. "Me, too. But you'll text me now and then, right?"

"Oh, yeah, sure. Because like all guys, I'm a great communicator."

She threw the shirt at him. "I have to shower."

Ten minutes later, she emerged from the bathroom and headed to her room. She assumed Andy had gone back to bed, but to her surprise, she found him standing at her dresser. His back was to her and he appeared to be fiddling with something.

"Did I forget to pack something?" she asked worriedly.

He started and turned around. She thought she saw

a look of guilt cross his face. But then he flashed her his lopsided grin, and she decided she was mistaken. He fished a pair of socks out of the top dresser drawer. "You'll need these, right?"

Helicity shrugged. "I've got five pairs already. Lana said that'd be plenty. But hand me my purse, will you? It's right there on the dresser."

Andy grabbed the purse and tossed it to her.

Helicity blinked. "Hey!" she cried. "You threw that with your right arm! Does that mean it's feeling better? That the rehab is working?"

Andy's brow furrowed. He flexed the fingers of his right hand, grimaced, and shook his head. "You know, for a second there, I didn't feel the pain. But now . . . it's back."

"Oh." Disappointment washed over her. She'd hoped to leave for her trip with the knowledge that he was mending. "You need me to get you something for it?"

"No, no, I'm trying to cut back on the meds."

He rolled his shoulder as if to test it out. His face suddenly creased with pain. He smiled weakly and sat on the bed. "Then again, maybe just one more. I didn't sleep very well last night. I keep having this bad dream about the accident."

"Sit," Helicity ordered. "I'll get it." She hurried to his room and retrieved the orange bottle of pain medication. It was half-full, she noted, and she figured her father must have gotten the refill he wanted after all. She gave the bottle to Andy, then picked up her suitcase and grabbed her purse from the bed.

"Whoops!" Her phone slipped out and hit the floor. Luckily, it landed on the carpet, so it was unharmed. "Shoot. I could have sworn I zipped that up."

"Must not have," Andy said.

She rolled her eyes. "Thank you, Captain Obvious."

Lana and Sam arrived two hours later. Helicity's parents had met with Lana earlier in the week to discuss exactly what Helicity would be doing, and to Helicity's relief, her father came away with a grudging respect for the meteorologist.

"She knows what she's doing, anyway," he said that night.

Sam, though, with his bad-boy appearance and

laid-back attitude, was a different story. He and Andy eyeballed one another with thinly veiled contempt, and her father and mother looked him up and down and exchanged troubled glances.

Lana must have picked up on the tension, for she ordered Sam to take Helicity's things to the car. He grabbed her suitcase and purse and headed outside. Lana made sure both Mr. and Mrs. Dunlap had her contact information, that day's itinerary, and the name of the hotel they were staying at that night. Then she left Helicity to say good-bye to her parents and brother in private.

"Be safe," her father said, giving her a quick kiss on the head. "And keep your cell phone charged. Right?" He ruffled her hair to show he was joking.

Andy wrapped her in a one-armed hug. "Tell that Sam guy that I'll come after him if—"

"I know, I know," Helicity said, rolling her eyes. But she smiled, too.

She embraced her mother last. "I love you, Mom," she whispered. "I wouldn't be going if it weren't for you."

"I love you, too, sweet thing. Come home to us safe

and sound, okay?" Her mother squeezed her hard one last time. Then Helicity broke free and hurried out to Lana's SUV. She climbed into the backseat. Lana started the engine.

And then they were off.

CHAPTER SEVENTEEN

The sun had been shining when Helicity got up that morning. Any other group of people heading off for a summer adventure would have assumed sunshine meant perpetual sunshine. Not Helicity, Lana, and Sam. They grinned at one another. They knew that heat was just what the atmosphere needed to start cooking up storms.

"It's a sign," Lana said. "Feel that heat, the dew point climbing?"

"Yes!" Sam and Helicity crowed together. Lana laughed.

"We have about an hour or so to kill before we reach the ferry," she said. "Perfect time to get to know one another better. First topic: Place you'd most like to visit. It can be anywhere in the world. Sam, you first."

"Easy," Sam replied. "Where the Catatumbo River meets Lake Maracaibo."

Lana laughed again. "Why am I not surprised?"

"Wait, Cata-what and Lake Mara-huh?" Helicity asked.

Sam regarded her with disbelief. "You, the weather wonder, have never heard of the Beacon of Maracaibo?"

Helicity shook her head.

Sam's eyes danced with excitement. "Catatumbo River flows into Lake Maracaibo in northern Venezuela. There's a swampy expanse where they join. Hot, moist air rises up from the swamp and meets the cooler air from the Andes Mountains." He diagrammed the meeting with his hands, sweeping one up to join the other. "And bam, thunderstorms break out."

Helicity shrugged. "I don't get it. That sort of thing happens in lots of places. What makes this spot so special?"

"Because the same thing happens two to three hundred nights a year. And every night it does, thousands of lightning bolts fill the sky for, like, ten hours."

Helicity's jaw dropped. "Get out. You're making that up."

"He's not," Lana affirmed. "I've been there."

"No way!" Sam cried. "What was it like?"

"Unbelievable. Wild. Unstable. Crackling with energy. Kind of like you, actually."

Sam preened. "I'll take that as a compliment."

"I'm stunned," Lana said sarcastically. "Okay, Helicity. What about you? Any place you've been dying to see?"

Helicity thought for a long moment. She wanted to choose something as exotic and noteworthy as Sam's lightning display, but kept coming back to one answer. "I've always wanted to see the aurora borealis," she finally confessed. "So Alaska or Norway or Iceland, I guess."

Lana nodded. "Good choice. The northern lights are well worth seeing."

Helicity dipped her head and blushed with pleasure.

"Your turn, Lana," Sam said. "Where to?"

"That's easy. There's a peninsula of land in eastern Massachusetts called Cape Cod. It juts out into the Atlantic Ocean. Looks like an arm making a muscle." She demonstrated with her arm. "Below the armpit area is the island of Martha's Vineyard. Great place for a vacation: beaches with huge waves, lots of bike trails, whale-watching excursions, and cute little towns with ice cream parlors, fudge and saltwater taffy stores, and little souvenir shops."

"Sounds like Mackinac," Sam commented, referring to a Michigan island in Lake Huron, north of the lower peninsula.

"Same sort of feel," Lana agreed, "except Martha's Vineyard and its sister island, Nantucket, are right out in the ocean, unprotected by any natural barriers. That makes them vulnerable to hurricanes and tropical storms. I was in one—Bob, August of '91."

"You were on the island during the hurricane?" Helicity gasped.

Lana nodded. "It was a cat two, the winds and waves caused tremendous destruction. Erosion to the southern shoreline. Weeklong power outages. Flooding.

Millions of dollars of damage to boats, homes, buildings."

"And *this* is the place you want to visit?" Sam asked incredulously. "Why?"

"It's the first place I experienced the power of weather," Lana explained. "One day, we were playing at the beach and strolling through the town. The next, monstrous waves pummeled that same beach and storm surge flooded the streets. A college girl died—hit by a truck. I remember it all so clearly." She caught Helicity's eye in the rearview mirror. "Martha's Vineyard is where I became a weather junkie. So yeah, I'd like to visit it again sometime before I die."

They arrived at the Muskegon ferry dock a short while later. A thin veil of clouds had taken over the sky, and humidity hung in the air, making Helicity feel sluggish and sticky when she got out of the car. So when Lana handed her a ticket for the ferry and told her to get on board, she was confused.

"Aren't you coming?"

Lana laughed. "I have to drive the SUV belowdecks.

You and Sam get us seats on the top, okay? That's where the best view is."

"Come on, Fourteen," Sam said. "Let's get in line."

Helicity followed him up the gangplank onto the ferry. A jolt of excitement ran up her spine and erased the fog from her mind. She'd been on boats before, but never one this big. And Lake Michigan—she'd seen it from shore and swum in it plenty of times, but it looked completely different from their top deck seats. Spread out before her, a vast expanse of dark blue and deep green with sun sparkles dancing on the surface, it seemed to have no end.

"It's so beautiful," she murmured as she pushed stray hair out of her face. "It's—"

Blaaaaaaaa!

A nearby horn gave a deafening blast. Helicity clapped her hands over her ears. Sam did the same. He nudged her with his elbow and grinned. She grinned back, then laughed out loud as the boat shuddered beneath them.

This is really happening, she thought as the ferry began moving. I'm going to be a storm chaser. And I'm going with Sam.

She could smell him again. It was a distinct smell that excited her almost as much as the adventure that had just begun.

A few minutes later, Lana appeared next to her. With her was an older black man with grizzled white-and-black hair and a potbelly. He looked oddly familiar, but it wasn't until Lana introduced him as her longtime storm-chasing buddy, Ray, that Helicity recognized him.

"You're the guy who cheated death!" she cried.

Ray laughed. "Lana still has that old newspaper clipping stuck to her bulletin board, huh?"

"Like I'd ever get rid of it," Lana replied, touching her lightning bolt necklace. "Ray, this is the girl I've been telling you about, Helicity Dunlap."

"Best name ever," Ray said, shaking Helicity's hand.

"Hi," Sam said. "I'm chopped liver, apparently. No, actually, I'm Sam. Sam Levesque."

Ray nodded. "My wingman. My wheels are parked down below. I call my ride Mo West, for Mobile Weather Station. Want to go check her out?"

"Heck yeah!" Sam cried. He and Ray disappeared down the stairs.

Helicity looked at Lana. "Wingman?"

"Ray has his own storm-chasing vehicle," Lana explained. "Sam will ride with him to our hotel. Hopefully, they won't kill each other because they're rooming together for the rest of the trip. Oh, and you'll be rooming with me," she added. "Okay?"

Helicity's heart filled to bursting at the thought of spending one-on-one time with her mentor. "Yeah," she said, eyes shining. "That's totally okay with me."

Lana smiled, then turned to gaze out at the lake. "You know, I have a good feeling about this trip." She leaned on the railing and tilted her head back to catch the sun on her face. "A real good feeling."

CHAPTER EIGHTEEN

JUNE 26

Madison, Wisconsin

I've never kept a journal before because let's face it—I've never had anything this exciting to record before!

So I'm here in Madison, sharing a hotel room with Lana. She says it's a two-star establishment, nothing great, and maybe it is a little run-down with peeling wallpaper and musty-smelling carpets. But who cares? We're only here for one night, then it's off to the next stop, Cedar Rapids, Iowa.

But that's tomorrow. Right now, my mind is buzzing

with what happened today. The drive with Sam and Lana (fun), the ferry ride across Lake Michigan (fun, then a little boring because it was so loooong!), then the wait with Sam while Lana and Ray got their SUVs off the boat (even loooooonger!!). Ray suggested pushing on to Dubuque, but that would have been another few hours driving, so Lana, Sam, and I outvoted him. And here we are.

Ray is super cool, by the way. I could listen to his storm-chasing stories for hours—especially those that Lana's in, which is most of them. They clearly adore each other, in a father-daughter kind of way.

Oh, jeez, that reminds me—Lana doesn't have any family! Her parents were killed in a fire when she was in college, and she's an only child. No aunts, no uncles, no living grandparents, either, and Ray was teasing her about being married to her work, so I guess that means she's never had a husband (or wife . . . whatever!). Basically, she's alone in the world except for Ray. And Sam and me now, too.

Oh, and the group that sponsored this trip, the LME Foundation? LME stands for Lana McElvoy. Apparently, she inherited a lot of money when her parents died. She used it to create the foundation, which helps fund science and engineering projects and stuff. Pretty cool, if you ask me.

Sam loves Ray—or at least, he loves Ray's SUV, Mo West. It is unbelievable. HUGE and totally tricked out with the best storm-chasing gear like ham radio equipment (made a fool of myself laughing about "ham"—duh), two mounted laptops for GPS and SAT radar, cameras and lenses, binoculars, and a bunch of other stuff. Sam is a tech geek (who knew?), and he and Ray were babbling about the software and gear all through dinner. (Snore.)

Anyway, Lana says I should turn in now. So good night!

JUNE 27
Cedar Rapids, Iowa

Another day of travel, this time about three and a half hours on the highway. Good cell phone service, even though it's raining. I called home, figuring Andy would be bored, but Mom picked up. She said

Andy wasn't feeling good, so she'd taken the day off from work to be with him. I started to ask what was wrong, but she had to hang up because he was calling for her. I'll try again later.

I texted with Mia a lot. She's loving Texas so far. Says her aunt is pretty easygoing compared to her mom. (Anyone would be—Mia's mom is wound up tighter than a drum.) The B-and-B has some guests, but no cute guys, so she's disappointed. (Typical Mia!) She asked if Sam had made a move on me yet. Yeah, right, as if!! I texted an eye-rolling emoji, she sent back one with hearts, and we had an all-out emoji war until she had to go clean one of the guest bathrooms. Ew.

It's been raining hard all day, and the desk clerk here at the hotel said it has been for three days straight. He sounded worried. Lana told me later that Cedar Rapids has had serious flooding problems in the past, so I guess that explains the guy's concern.

I wonder if I should be worried, too.

JUNE 28

Quick note from the road

Up early. Heading north, following the storm. Strong winds. Ray and Sam are up ahead. Lana's eyes are glued to their taillights. I'm watching for changes to the clouds and precipitation.

This is real. . . .

JUNE 29

Charles City, Iowa

Yesterday was crazy! We followed the storm for a while, but nothing besides rain and wind developed, so after a few hours, we called it quits.

We were all hungry, so we stopped at a diner for lunch. While we were waiting for our order, Ray saw a brief radar-indicated tornado . . . we got in the car and rushed that way, but it was gone almost as soon as we turned out of the diner. We were bummed—Sam in particular—because if we'd kept going we might have seen it. But that's how it is sometimes. The local storm report said it had been spotted, only briefly, by a local farmer.

That wasn't the crazy part, though. We went back to the diner to actually eat and just as our food came out—BANG! High winds sent a tree crashing onto the hood of Lana's SUV! The damage made it undrivable, so she had it towed to a nearby car shop. Unfortunately, it might not be ready for a day or two because a lot of the workers are already gone for the Fourth of July (almost forgot that holiday was coming up!). We can't all fit in Ray's truck, so Lana and Ray checked us into this hotel. They went to talk to the farmer. Sam and I stayed behind.

The rain let up later in the afternoon, so Sam and I swam in the outdoor pool, then walked to get ice cream at Dairy Queen. It was fun until I went to pay. That's when I discovered some of my money was missing—forty dollars, to be exact! I *know* I put the whole seventy-five in my wallet before I left home, and I haven't spent any since the trip began because Lana's been paying for everything. Sam says maybe some hotel worker took the cash, but I don't think so because I've had my purse with me all the time.

I don't know. Maybe I did leave some at home. I'll
ask Andy to look the next time I call. Hopefully, he'll be
feeling better by then.

So all that happened yesterday. It's morning now,
and Lana and Ray left an hour ago to follow up on the
farmer's claim—seems they think he might have been
wrong or even lying to get insurance money or
something. They want to take some more pictures of
the damage. Sam and I said we didn't mind cramming
into the back of the SUV, but apparently the farmer is
pretty ornery (Ray's word, not mine!) and Lana wasn't too
keen on us being around him.

So Sam and I are stuck here at the hotel again. It's
pouring out, so no leaving the hotel to walk around town
and no indoor pool. If we don't find something to do
besides watch TV and wait for Lana and Ray to return, I
think we'll go crazy!!

CHAPTER NINETEEN

Helicity finished her entry and closed her journal with a heavy sigh. Sam was stretched out on Lana's bed, watching a news report about concerns of flooding in vulnerable areas of the state. Suddenly, the room phone rang, startling them both.

"Should we answer it?" Helicity asked.

Sam shrugged and picked up the receiver. He spoke for a few minutes, then hung up. "That was the front desk. The repair shop just dropped off Lana's car. Come on, let's go check it out, make sure it's okay."

Grateful for any excuse to get out of the room, Helicity followed Sam to the elevator. Downstairs, the desk clerk seemed reluctant to hand over the keys until Sam pointed out the SUV was blocking the main entrance.

"You can move it yourself if you like," he added with a careless shrug. "But then you'd have to run through the rain to get back inside. You really want to finish your shift in wet clothes and messy hair?"

The clerk didn't need more convincing. She slid the keys over to Sam.

"Come on, Fourteen," Sam said. They pushed through the revolving door.

Helicity didn't think it was possible, but the rain had intensified since they'd left the room. It pounded on the entrance overhang, gushed out the ends of the metal downspouts, and fell in sheets beyond the covering. A blast of wind flung wet spray at Helicity. Impatient to get in the car, she yelled at Sam. "Hey, stop fiddling with your phone and open up, will you? I'm getting soaked!"

The locks clicked. She yanked the passenger side door open and jumped in. Sam did the same. His black hair was wet and stuck to his face, but he didn't seem to notice. Grinning like a madman, he tossed his phone in the cup holder, jammed the key in the ignition, and started the engine.

"Lights." He flicked on the headlights. "Camera." He turned on Lana's dash cam. "And . . . action." He hit the gas. But instead of driving to the parking area, he turned out of the lot and onto the road.

"Hey, wait!" Helicity cried over the rapid thump of the windshield wipers. "What are you doing?"

"Got an alert," Sam replied gleefully. "Possible tornado fifteen miles south of here."

"So? We can't just go off and—"

"And chase it?" Sam laughed. "Helicity, you're kidding, right? That's what we're here to do!"

"But what about Lana and Ray? We have to tell them!"

"So go ahead and text them! They probably saw the warning too and are on their way right now!" He pressed the accelerator. The SUV surged forward through a wide puddle, sending up a wall of dirty brown water.

Helicity's insides twisted as she pulled out her phone and sent Lana a text. What Sam was doing was reckless. She'd never been more sure of anything in her life. But she knew nothing she said would convince him to turn around.

Should I make him pull over and let me out? she thought as the SUV swung around another corner. She rejected the idea immediately. *I let him go after a storm alone once before. Never again. He needs another pair of eyes to get through this safely.*

She opened her GPS app. "Tell me where we're going," she said through gritted teeth, "and I'll get us there."

Traffic on the main road out of town was thin but slow moving because of the driving rain. On one straight stretch, Sam accelerated to veer around a sedan. As they passed the car, the driver shot Helicity a dirty look. She didn't blame him.

"How much farther?" Sam asked.

"Turn left, then it's just—"

"Left where? Here? Or the one up ahead?"

"Here—no, wait! The next one!" Helicity flung out her arms to brace herself as Sam jerked the wheel one way, then back again. Her phone slipped from her hand and fell at her feet.

"Come on, Fourteen, work with me here, huh?" Sam growled.

He took the correct turn onto a one-car lane that bisected two massive cornfields. No other vehicles were in sight.

Helicity leaned down to retrieve her phone. Suddenly, a large truck roared out from a side road hidden by the corn. Sam slammed on the brakes. Helicity's head struck the dashboard with a dull thud. She saw stars.

"Whoa, you okay, Fourteen?"

Heart hammering in her chest, Helicity rubbed the painful spot and nodded. The truck was on the same road up ahead of them now. She peered through the windshield and read the logo on the back: *Tornado Tom, Seeker of Storms.*

She sucked in her breath. "Tornado Tom. I've seen that guy's videos. He's, like, the superstar of storm chasers."

Sam gripped the wheel more tightly. "Then that means we're heading in the right direction. But unless I can get around him, he'll get there first." He nosed the SUV to the left as if preparing to pass.

"Wait, Sam, don't! There isn't enough room!"

Sam kept going. The SUV's left tires grazed the edge of the cornfield, snapping stalks and crushing them. Helicity pressed her hands on the dashboard, willing Sam to drop back. But he pressed on, pumping his fist and giving a loud whoop when he zoomed by Tornado Tom's truck.

"Oh, yeah, baby! There's a new chaser in town, and his name is Sam Levesque!"

They drove for another half mile with Tom close behind. Then all at once, Tom started honking his horn. Helicity looked in her side-view mirror, expecting to see the truck closing in. To her consternation, it had come to a halt and was flashing its lights at them, still honking.

Too late, Helicity understood Tom was trying to warn them. She looked at her GPS and gasped. "Stop!" she yelled.

The cornfields ended abruptly, cut off by a wide stream that formed a T with their road. A long one-vehicle wooden bridge crossed the stream. In fair weather, it would have been a pretty spot— waving fields of corn, wide blue sky, and cool, clear water flowing below the wooden structure.

Now, though, that flow was a swift-moving flood that swamped the bridge's surface and the roadway around it.

Sam braked hard. They pitched forward in their seats. Helicity made a strangled sound in her throat as her seat belt dug into her shoulder and chest. But the SUV didn't stop. The water covering the road was just an inch or two deep, but that was enough to separate the tires from the pavement. They started hydroplaning, skidding out of control across the water's surface.

"Hang on!" Sam shouted, his voice frantic with fear.

The SUV careened onto the bridge, fishtailed sideways, and slammed into the wooden rails. The airbags deployed. Helicity screamed as the rails gave way. They tilted over the side—and hung there. For a split second, she dared to think they were safe.

Then the wood holding them groaned and snapped. They nosedived into the water. The SUV's grille hit the streambed with a sickening crunch of metal on rock. The windshield blew apart.

And then the water started to pour in.

CHAPTER TWENTY

"**S**am! We've got to get out of here!" Helicity screamed. Miraculously, the engine was still running. She hit the window button, and as it rolled down, she unbuckled and started to climb out. Then she realized Sam hadn't moved.

"Oh, God. *Sam!*" He was slumped over the airbag. There was blood and broken glass in his hair. She swung back in, undid his seat belt, and as quickly and gently as she could, pushed him back against the seat.

For one heart-stopping moment, she thought he was dead. Then he blinked and stared at her, dazed. "Wha-what's happening?" A splash of water caught him in the face. It seemed to clear his focus. His face turned into a rictus of horror. "Oh my God!"

"Come *on!*" Helicity lunged over him and slammed her palm on the window control. The pane of glass slid slowly down into the door. She twisted the key and turned off the engine. "Use the roof rack bars to climb up! *Now!*"

Sam did as she ordered, slithering through the opening. His legs were disappearing when she moved back to her window. She reached up and out, feeling for the roof rack rails. She touched them. Her wet fingers slipped, then found purchase. Torquing her body awkwardly through the opening and using her legs to push, she hauled herself out and then pulled up next to Sam.

Panting, they stared at each other. Blood trickled down Sam's face from a deep gash on his forehead. His eyes were full of despair.

"Fourteen," he choked, "I—"

"Hey! Hey, you kids!"

A deep baritone shout as penetrating as a foghorn bellowed out to them. They turned their heads, moving cautiously so as not to shift the SUV from its tenuous position. Tornado Tom stood at the edge of the water. He'd parked so his truck was facing them. He held two bright orange life vests. Another man was feverishly unwinding cable from a winch attached to the truck's grille.

Tom clipped the life vests to the cable with a heavy-duty carabiner. He cupped his hands around his mouth. "Get ready to catch!"

It took three throws before the vests reached them. Helicity unclipped them, shoved one over her head and the other over Sam's. Then she started to attach the line to the roof rack.

"No!" Tom yelled. "Around yourself!" He mimed looping the cable under his arms and fastening the clip. "We'll pull you in one at a time!"

"Okay!" Helicity yelled back. She inched toward Sam.

He drew back. "You first!"

"No! You're hurt! You need help more than me!" She didn't wait for him to argue, encircling him with the cable and securing the clip.

He grabbed her hand. "If you don't make it—"

"I will! I'm a survivor!" She squeezed his hand and shouted, "Go!" to Tom.

The winch started turning. The line tightened. Sam was pulled away from her. At the last second, he released her hand and fell into the water. His head disappeared for a second. Then he bobbed back up and the winch started dragging him through the current. When he neared the water's edge, Tom splashed in and dragged him out.

His partner immediately unclipped the line and threw it to Helicity. It soared overhead. She reached up to snatch it from the air but missed. It snagged on a bar on the far side of the SUV. She slowly crawled over, trying not to imagine the vehicle shifting underneath her, and tugged to free the line.

"Helicity!"

A scream cut through the driving rain and howling wind like a knife. Helicity looked over her shoulder to see Lana and Ray leaping out of Ray's truck.

Helicity gave a sob of relief. "I'm okay!" she cried. "I—"

"Hurry!" Lana shrieked. *"Oh my God, Helicity— hurry!"*

That's when Helicity detected a faint sound in the distance—a dull rumble, like faraway thunder.

But she knew in an instant that it wasn't thunder.

It had been raining hard in northern Iowa for days. Swollen streams and rivers were threatening to crest their banks and overtop hastily constructed sandbag walls and breach levees. But that colossal wall of water could still break through the barricades. If it did, it would churn and pound downstream with incredible speed. And it would sound like thunder.

A flash flood.

If she was right, one of the most powerful and destructive forces of nature was hurtling toward her. If she was caught in it, no life vest would save her. She'd be swept away, her body hurled against hidden rocks, battered by downed trees and branches and other debris. That pummeling might not kill her, but it could knock her out. She'd be pulled beneath the white water . . . and then she would drown.

I have to get to high ground now.

With one fierce yank, she freed the cable. "Pull!" she yelled as she looped it around herself and fastened the clip. The winch tugged her into the water. She came up gasping, the cold water stealing the breath from her lungs. Ray, Tom, his partner, and Lana hauled on the line, pulling her faster than the winch. Helicity kicked, but the swift-moving water fought against her, sapping her strength so each movement became weaker and weaker.

Suddenly, Lana froze and turned upstream. *"No!"* She dropped the line, ran into the water, grabbed Helicity's vest, and began hauling her backward.

"Come on, darling, you can do this. Help me do this," Lana begged. Helicity clutched Lana's shirt, dug her feet into the slick mud beneath her, and with her last bit of strength, pushed.

At that same instant, the men gave a sharp pull. Helicity surged forward unexpectedly and knocked Lana off her feet. Helicity tightened her grasp on Lana's shirt. The current rolled them so she ended staring up into Lana's eyes.

Time stood still. Then Lana's lips moved. Helicity tried to make out the words. But she couldn't hear anything but the pounding water.

The men yanked again. Helicity lost her grip on Lana's shirt and shot backward, sliding effortlessly over the slippery muck. One more yank and Tom's partner was dragging her to higher ground. She fought him, sobbing and struggling to see past him to the water.

"Lana. *Lana!*"

Lana scrambled upright and thrashed toward her. She was fast.

But the thundering wall of water was faster.

A FORCE OF NATURE . . . A FORCE OF DEATH

Helicity stared at the video title on Tornado Tom's website. Her fingertip grazed the touch pad and shifted the cursor to PLAY. She hesitated, then tapped the arrow.

The screen changed to an image of a sky thick with dark, billowing clouds. "If you think flash floods can't hurt you," Tornado Tom's solemn voice-over intoned, "think again."

A lightning bolt cut a brilliant zigzag through the gray. A monstrous clap of thunder made her speakers tremble. Tom appeared on the screen, a grave expression on his craggy face.

"The following video, taken just days ago from my dash cam, shows graphic images of the destructive power of flash floods." His voice dropped to an even more somber tone. "It also shows just how life-threatening that power can be."

The video shifted to the rain-soaked windshield of Tornado Tom's storm-chasing truck. The image blurred briefly, then refocused through the glass.

Helicity's breath caught in her throat. There was Lana's SUV, dangling nose-first from the narrow wooden bridge, its grille buried in the surging river below. Sam clung to the rooftop. Rainwater mingled with the blood dripping from his head wound. Seconds later, she watched herself struggle out of the far side of the SUV.

She hit FAST FORWARD, moving quickly past Sam's rescue, her fumbling attempts to free the tow rope, and her fall into the cold rushing water. She pressed PLAY when Lana loomed into view.

"No!"

Lana's scream of horror was muffled by the driving

rain, rushing water, and windshield, but it still cut through Helicity like a knife. Her vision swam as Lana plunged into the churning waves to save her.

"Hey! Enough of that!"

She started. Andy stood in her bedroom doorway. Frowning, he moved to her bedside and shut her laptop. "Enough of that," he repeated, more gently this time but with a finality that brooked no argument.

Helicity slumped back against a wall of pillows and winced in pain. As soft as the pillows were, she still felt the bruises that bloomed in ugly shades of purple, blue, and black across her torso and arms. Whether the injuries were from the SUV crash or the violent pulls on the tow rope, she didn't know. Didn't care.

"She almost died because of me."

Andy sank onto the bed next to her. "The key word there is *almost*."

Helicity looked at her brother with tortured eyes. "When I was in the hospital, I heard the nurses talking. They thought I was asleep, but I heard them. They said—"

Her voice caught. She swallowed hard. "They said rescuers found her body a mile downstream.

It . . . she . . . was battered. Broken. Barely alive."

"But she *is* alive, Hel. *That's* what you have to focus on!"

"She's in a coma, Andy! What if she never comes out of it?"

Andy was quiet for a long moment. Then he glanced over his shoulder and, in a low voice, said, "Would it help if you saw her?"

Helicity sat up. "What? How?"

"They moved her here, to our hospital, a few days ago."

Fury rocked her. "And no one told me?"

Andy held up his hand. "Hey, you weren't in such good shape a few days ago. Plus, I don't know if you're allowed to visit her because you're not family."

"She doesn't *have* family," Helicity growled.

Andy went on as if she hadn't spoken. "Even if they have that policy, I have connections at the hospital, people who looked out for me when I was there. I've stayed in touch with a few of them." He glanced over his shoulder again. "I can get you in."

"Let's go." Helicity shoved her laptop aside and climbed off the bed. As she did, Lana's necklace swung free from her shirt. The lightning bolt charm winked in the sunlight.

The necklace had come off in her hand when she lost her grip on Lana's shirt. She'd clutched it all the way to the hospital, refusing to part with it, lashing out like a wild animal whenever anyone tried to take it from her.

Anyone except Ray. The big bear of a man with his deep, warm laugh and never-ending stories had aged twenty years overnight—and turned as silent as the grave. He came to see her soon after she left the hospital. She'd given him the necklace then. But instead of pocketing it, he kissed her on the forehead and placed it around her neck.

"Hang on to it for her," he murmured. "Give it back when she comes to, okay?"

She hadn't taken it off since.

She tucked the lightning bolt back inside her shirt, then loosened her braid and reached for her comb. It lay on her dresser next to an orange bottle of pain pills. Her doctor had prescribed them "just in case." She'd taken one the first night. But the drug had given her such disturbing dreams that she'd left the rest of the pills untouched. The over-the-counter medication wasn't as strong, but she preferred the minor pain to the prescription pill's side effects.

Andy's reflection joined hers in the mirror. His gaze flicked to the dresser top. A ghost of a smile crossed his face. It vanished when he saw her watching him. He murmured that he'd meet her in the car and left.

Helicity bit her lip. Andy had been acting odd lately. Outwardly, he appeared to be mending. His bruises had faded and his cuts had healed, and while his arm was still bound, he didn't seem to be holding it as gingerly. But something wasn't right. He was secretive and reclusive. To Helicity, it was as if something inside him was broken. What, she didn't know.

She'd also detected an undercurrent of uneasiness in her household. Her parents seemed to be walking on eggshells around each other, and even more strangely, around Andy.

She shook her head. Whatever was going on, she wasn't going to have to live with it for much longer. In two weeks, she'd be on a plane to Texas.

Mia had reached out to her the first moment she could, inviting her to come stay with her at the bed-and-breakfast. To Helicity's surprise, her parents readily agreed to let her go. "It will be good for you to be away from . . . reminders," her mother had said.

How much time she'd spend in Texas was up to her. She had a one-way ticket, so she could return whenever she chose.

She and Andy entered the hospital ten minutes later. Members of the staff greeted them with polite nods. A few did double takes when she passed, no doubt recognizing her from the news coverage of the accident. She guessed what they were thinking: how horrific it was that a woman had nearly died because of her. How guilty she must feel to be walking about while her rescuer lay unconscious. How tragic it would be if her savior died without ever waking. She guessed, because it was what she herself was thinking.

She tightened her lips, wrapped her hand around the lightning bolt, and followed Andy down the corridor. Hospital smells assaulted her nose—ammonia, institutional food, vomit. She didn't register the path they took, but suddenly, she was standing in front of a window outside of Lana's room.

"Come on." Andy ushered her inside. "If you're

lucky, you'll have a few minutes before they start asking questions or kick you out." He pulled out his phone. "Text me when you're through."

"Where will you be?"

"With a friend. I'll find you." He left, his thumbs moving over his phone as he typed a text. The door closed behind him with a gentle shushing sound.

Helicity stood rooted to the spot for a long moment. Now that she was here, she couldn't look at Lana. Not yet. Instead, she read the cards sent from well-wishers—her parents, Pete, Tornado Tom, and a few other storm chasers, and Ray, of course. But one person's name was missing.

Helicity hadn't seen Sam since the tragedy. She knew he'd been checked into the hospital with her. But he, and his baby-blue sedan, had disappeared soon after he was released. Every now and then, Helicity thought about texting him. But she never did. She simply had nothing to say to him. And she was worried about what he would have to say to her. They had made a bad decision together, and the result lay in the bed behind her.

She read the last card, then took a deep breath and

slowly turned to face Lana. The storm chaser was lying in bed. Wires ran from blinking, beeping machines to sensors on her arms and head. A tube snaked between her lips, which looked cracked and painfully dry. That tube was breathing for her, Helicity realized. Lana's eyes were closed.

"Oh, Lana." Swallowing back tears, Helicity drew up a chair. She wanted to take Lana's hand but didn't dare. Lana looked fragile and swollen, no longer the bold and brave hero Helicity had grown to adore. Instead, she rested her hand on the covers so her pinkie touched Lana's.

"Please wake up," she whispered. "Please."

Lana's eyes stayed closed, the only sound outside Helicity's muffled tears, the consistent beep from Lana's heart rate monitor.

Helicity was silent on the ride home. Inside, she changed into her riding outfit of jeans, long-sleeved shirt, and boots. She wheeled an old bike she'd found in the rental house garage and pedaled to the farm where Raven was stabled. The bicycle was too small, and her growing legs crunched to her chest as she fought through tears again. The bike, like so much of the rest of her life since the accident, just didn't fit.

The sun was lowering in the sky, turning the wispy cirrus clouds on the horizon into flames of red, orange, and yellow, as she rode her horse up the hill. She climbed onto the boulder, sat down and drew her knees into her chest, and tilted her head back to stare at the sky. Tears leaked from the corners of her eyes and trailed down her jawline as she thought about Lana lying in the hospital bed.

But after a minute, she stood and dashed the tears away. They didn't seem right, not when it came to Lana.

Because she's a survivor, she thought. Not a victim.

She stood up and tugged the necklace from beneath her shirt. She held the lightning bolt out with both hands like an offering to the setting sun.

She thought, *I'm going to get through this too.*

TURN THE PAGE
FOR A SNEAK PEEK
OF THE SEQUEL

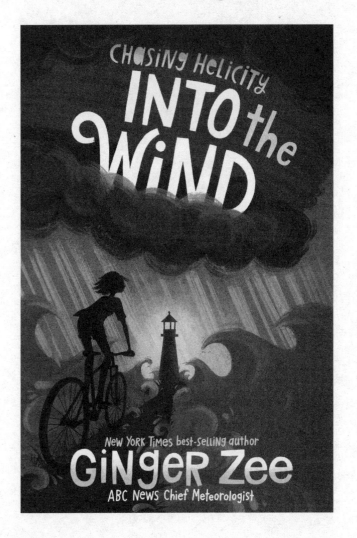

CHASING HELICITY

INTO the WIND

New York Times best-selling author

GINGER ZEE

ABC News Chief Meteorologist

CHAPTER ONE

"So, Felicity, are you ready for your first flight?"

Helicity Dunlap suppressed a sigh and turned to the woman in the severely starched airline uniform sitting beside her. JULIE, her name tag said. An airline chaperone, she was in charge of Helicity for the duration of the flight from Grand Rapids to Houston. There, she would hand her off to Helicity's best friend, Mia, and Mia's aunt. Julie seemed nice enough, even if she hadn't gotten her name right.

"It's *Hel*icity," she said patiently. "With an *H*."

Julie peeked at Helicity's paperwork. "Huh. I

assumed that was a typo, just another airline mistake. You know, like the food." She changed her voice to sound like a cheesy stand-up comedian. "Airline food—what's up with that?"

Helicity cringed inwardly at her chaperone's attempted humor. Outwardly, she offered Julie a polite smile.

Julie resumed her normal voice. "*Helicity*. I've never heard that before. Is it a family name?"

Helicity was as used to this question as she was to people getting her name wrong, so she had a ready answer. "My grandmother was a physicist. She studied helicity. I got the name because my mom liked the sound of the word, which means to spin, basically." The real definition of *helicity* was much more complex, but she'd learned long ago not to elaborate. Most people tended to glaze over when she did.

Further discussion was cut short by the announcement that the plane was ready for takeoff.

Julie grinned. "Here we go!"

The engines powered up with a high-pitched whine. A second later, the plane shot forward down the runway. As the G-force from the rapid acceleration pushed her back into her seat, Helicity instinctively reached for the necklace she always wore—a lightning bolt on a long chain. It wasn't hers; it belonged to her mentor, Lana McElvoy. Lana, who was still in a coma in a hospital. Because of her. Because of Helicity.

Her hand tightened around the charm's jagged edges as the wheels bumped on the tarmac. Then the wheels left the earth behind, and the plane soared on a sharp incline into the sky.

Helicity pushed aside her bangs and curled up closer to the small oval window. She had recently given herself a super short, shoulder-length bob haircut that swept across her forehead. She'd done a decent job, but the new style made her look much older, and her mother had been startled when she saw it. Helicity had needed to make the change, just as she'd needed to take her horse, Raven, for long solo rides in the countryside surrounding her hometown and to travel hundreds of miles to Texas. Anything and everything to avoid running into her past.

Outside the window, the ground below vanished in a shroud of pale gray mist.

I'm inside a cloud, Helicity realized.

Seconds later, the plane burst through the foggy layer and into the brilliant blue sky above. She blinked at the sudden brightness. Then her eyes adjusted, and her breath caught in her throat.

A carpet of puffy stratocumulus clouds stretched in endless waves toward the horizon. The late afternoon sunshine painted the expanse with warm golden tones. The only thing missing from the fairy-tale landscape was a palace gleaming in the distance.

Helicity was enthralled. She loved anything to do with clouds. Anything to do with the weather in general, in fact, which was why she dreamed of becoming a meteorologist and storm chaser one day. While many kids her age spent their free time staring at screens, Helicity scanned the world around her for evidence of atmospheric and environmental change. Things like trees bending in the wind and grassy fields parched to brown from lack of rain. Shimmering heat creating that beautiful mirage, radiating up from the pavement, and sunlight softened by low-hanging haze. Slick patches of black ice lying in wait for unwary travelers and powdery snow skimming across frozen expanses. Each day, the ever-changing conditions delivered something new and amazing, and Helicity didn't want to miss a single moment.

Or at least, that's how she felt until two terrifying storms—first a tornado, then a flash flood—caught her and those she loved in their powerful clutches. Her parents had lost everything in the tornado. Her brother, Andy, had risked his life to search for her during that same terrible storm. And Lana—

"It's beautiful, isn't it?"

Julie broke into Helicity's thoughts. Helicity blinked, then lifted a shoulder and let it drop. "Oh, yeah . . . it's nice."

"I've seen views like that hundreds of times," Julie continued. "One of the perks of working for the airline, you know?"

Helicity knew Julie was trying to engage her in conversation. But since the flood, she hadn't been sleeping well, and she just didn't have the energy to feign interest in small talk. So, after offering the chaperone a smile and a nod, she closed her eyes, intending to pretend she'd dozed off.

Soon, though, the plane's gentle rocking motion

and the steady drone of the engines lulled her into her first real sleep in weeks.

It didn't last long. The nightmares intruded, a familiar montage of disturbing images, some real, some fabricated by her overactive mind. Her mother cowering in the basement as the tornado ripped their home apart. Her father staring in anguish at his son's battered body. Lana mouthing something Helicity couldn't hear over the roar of the floodwaters. Andy wide-eyed with terror as his car flipped, rolled, bounced—

She woke with a gasp. The bouncing was no dream.

Turbulence. The word flashed through her mind as the plane gave another shudder.

Turbulence, she knew, was caused by sudden changes in the airflow around the plane, like a jetty in the ocean that disrupts the flow of ocean waters. Turbulence could be caused by so many different factors: nearby storms, proximity to mountain ranges, and alterations in the jet stream. There weren't any mountains nearby, and she didn't see any thunderstorms, so it had to be clear-air turbulence.

Knowing what caused the plane to shake was one

thing. Experiencing that shaking was something very different.

The shuddering stopped, then began again, more intensely this time. A tone sounded, and the FASTEN SEAT BELT sign flashed on. A finger of unease crawled up Helicity's spine. "Is this normal?" she asked Julie.

A lurch sent the chaperone's drink splashing into her lap. "Oh, sh—sugar," she amended in mid-expletive. She mopped at the mess with her tiny airline napkin, then shoved the sodden wad into her plastic cup. "I'll be right back."

Ignoring the seat belt sign, she unbuckled and headed to the galley. Suddenly, the plane gave a violent jerk. Julie stumbled. Helicity was thrown sideways in her seat. Her head hit the window, and she saw stars. When her vision cleared, she saw Julie had strapped herself into the plane's jump seat.

The loudspeaker crackled. "Ladies and gentlemen," the pilot calmly intoned, "as you have no doubt noticed, we are experiencing a bit of turbulence. At this time, we ask—"

His request was cut short when the plane suddenly plummeted like an elevator in freefall. Cries of alarm filled the cabin as Helicity and the other passengers went weightless for a split second. Then, like a yo-yo reaching the end of its string, the descent halted abruptly. Helicity nearly bit her tongue when she thudded back down into her seat.

Without warning, an overhead compartment popped open. A child's pink backpack tumbled out and hit the man sitting below. Cursing, he kicked it under the seat in front of him, then half-stood, twisting awkwardly to re-secure the latch.

"Sir! Sit down!" the attendant commanded.

Too late! The plane lurched again. The man flew backward into the aisle. A second jolt sent him sprawling forward. His nose cracked against the metal armrest. He howled and clapped a hand over his face. Blood gushed between his fingers and down his chin as he dragged himself back into his seat.

Helicity's fear spiked. She gripped the lightning bolt with both hands. Her palms were slick with sweat, but her mouth was bone-dry, her breath coming in ragged gasps.

I'm a survivor, not a victim. I'm a survivor, not a victim.

Out of nowhere, her mind conjured up the mantra that had pulled her back from the brink in the past. Some people might use the words *survivor* and *victim* interchangeably, but to her, their meanings were very different. Survivors pushed their way through adversity; victims were defined by it. Given a choice, she'd choose to be a survivor every time.

She latched on to the words, willing them to force out the adrenaline-fueled panic pulsing through her system. She breathed as Lana had once taught her, slow and deep, in through her nose and out through her mouth. She focused on the necklace digging into her palm—a sensation she could control and that could ground her.

I'm a survivor, not a victim.

The whine of the engines sliced into her thoughts. The plane nosed higher into the sky, aiming to rise above the turbulence. She sensed the passengers around her holding their breath. The craft jostled a few more times. Then, finally, the ride smoothed out.

A murmur of relief washed through the cabin.

"Who says Disney has the best rides?" the pilot

joked over the loudspeaker. His comment elicited a smattering of shaky, forced laughter.

Helicity slowly released her death grip on the necklace.

Julie hurried down the aisle. "You all right, Fel—*Hel*icity? I hope you weren't scared."

A sunbeam struck the lightning bolt, making it wink and flash.

"No, I wasn't scared," she murmured. *I was terrified.*